ADAM
CANFIELD
OF THE *DASH*

ADAM CANFIELD
OF THE *DASH*

MICHAEL WINERIP

WALKER BOOKS
AND SUBSIDIARIES

LONDON · BOSTON · SYDNEY · AUCKLAND

First published 2005 by Walker Books Ltd
87 Vauxhall Walk, London SE11 5HJ

2 4 6 8 10 9 7 5 3 1

Text © 2005 Michael Winerip
Cover illustration © 2005 Phil Schramm

This book has been typeset in Slimbach

Printed and bound in Great Britain by Cox & Wyman Ltd, Reading, Berkshire

British Library Cataloguing in Publication Data:
a catalogue record for this book is available
from the British Library

ISBN 1-84428-225-2

www.walkerbooks.co.uk

For Ben, Sam, Adam, Annie and Barney

chapter 1

Room 306

"All right," Jennifer was saying. "Ideas, ideas, and ideas. For the October issue. First issue of the new school year."

She waited. "We want it to be great."

She paused. "Anybody got anything?"

Silence. "Hello? I'm begging."

Adam found a spot on one of the sofas and flopped down just in time to see Jennifer shoot him a nasty look. What was the big deal? He wasn't that late. He had just wanted to put away his baritone horn before the meeting. Was it his fault his locker was on the first floor?

Adam loved the *Dash*, the student newspaper of Harris Elementary-Middle School. Ever since he was a cub reporter way back in third grade, room 306 was the one place in school—in his entire life, really—where he could sit back and let his mind go.

He glanced around. The room looked great. Same old filthy sofas covered with hot chocolate and iced-tea stains. Over the summer, somebody had ripped down the music and skateboard posters from the walls and computer terminals, but that didn't matter; they'd put up a new batch. A good turnout for the first meeting, too, practically every seat taken.

Still, he could tell, Jennifer was not happy. People were finally suggesting stories, but the ideas were really boring: Halloween safety tips from the Tremble police; the Dental Association was sponsoring a smile contest to promote Dental Health Month; the health sciences teacher had sent over a news release reminding students that the Say No to Drugs Community Players were holding fall auditions ("All Newcomers Welcome!").

Some third grader kept saying she wanted to do a story about Eddie the janitor. Adam couldn't believe it. Eddie the janitor?

He was slipping into a basketball daydream

when he felt a sting on his forehead. A spitball! He glanced up. Jennifer was waving a straw at him. "I'm not running this alone," she said. "We're coeditors, remember? What do *you* think?"

At that moment Adam was thinking maybe he had made a serious mistake. Jennifer had sworn she would not run the *Dash* this year unless someone helped her, and Adam had agreed to—sort of. But now Adam was thinking that maybe he should have stuck with being a star reporter. Maybe being in charge would take the fun out of the *Dash*. Maybe this was going to make the newspaper like everything else in his overprogrammed life—deadly serious.

He had to admit, it wasn't all Jennifer's fault; she did have her good points. Although they'd both been at Harris since kindergarten, and he'd seen her around the *Dash,* they'd never actually spoken much until last year. On that first day last September, he had rushed into class, late of course, grabbed the only available seat, and found himself next to Jennifer. She'd leaned over and whispered, "I was sure I was going to be the fastest one getting my work done this year. Then you come in, and I go, 'Uh-oh.'"

That was the nicest thing a girl had ever said to Adam, and it made him feel like he had a reputation at Harris. Yes, Jennifer definitely had her good points. As far as Adam was concerned, she had a sharp eye for talent, and she wasn't one of those annoying girls who spent all their time on the computer filling in do-it-yourself romance sites for boys they liked.

The thing about Jennifer, though—as Adam had tried to explain to her when she asked him to be her coeditor—was that the two of them were very different. She had a classic editor's personality. Steady, dependable, good at punctuation and that kind of stuff. Didn't mind being indoors a lot, tons of patience for nurturing artistic types.

Adam, on the other hand, as he had tried to make clear, was destined to live life on the edge. "I need to be on the streets, digging up dirt, taking dangerous risks for the public good."

"Oh, come on, just do it," she'd said, smiling at him.

"OK," he'd said. He had to admit, Jennifer had a pretty good smile.

Adam tried to focus.

"Hey, I want to write about Eddie the janitor." That third grader was squeaking again. All third graders looked alike to him—little and jittery. Usually they sat in the back and felt lucky to have a middle schooler talk to them. This one seemed to have the potential to be really annoying.

Adam figured this was the perfect opportunity to show Jennifer he was taking his coeditorship seriously. He hopped off the sofa. "All right," he said, "what about Eddie?" Adam had been at this school since day one of kindergarten and could not think of a single thing about the man that was remotely newsworthy, unless you considered pushing a wide broom down the hall for 150 years exciting. Adam figured an important part of being coeditor was nipping bad story ideas in the bud, and he was going to nip this one fast.

"He saved two baby birds who fell out of a nest," the third grader said. "They already had bugs crawling on them."

Adam stared at her.

"He's real nice," she said.

"What's your name, kid?" Adam asked. It was Phoebe. Adam wasn't surprised; she looked like a Phoebe, a real moochie-pie type. "Look," he said, trying to let a third grader down easy. "Let's put that idea on hold. Eddie the janitor is what we in the news biz call an *evergreen*. You might want to write that word in your notebook. E-V-E-R-G-R-E-E-N. Did I go too fast? It's a feature story that can run anytime. If we're having a slow month, trying to fill the paper, Eddie the janitor might be great. It could go on the back page, maybe with a small head shot. But this is the first issue of the new year. We want to— you know—kick a little butt."

Instantly, a sofa full of large middle-school boys began swaying and chanting, "Kick a little butt, get down tonight. Kick a little butt, get down tonight."

Adam acknowledged his audience, then he motioned for quiet. "Here's my idea," he said. "We create a Spotlight Team to investigate the cafeteria food."

Room 306 lit up like the Christmas tree at Rockefeller Center the day after Thanksgiving.

"We could find out why the hot dogs are green!" said a boy.

"We could drop them out a third-floor window— see how high they bounce," said another.

"Rubber! Rubber! Rubber!" chanted the boys, flopping around on the sofa like green hot dogs.

They wanted to see if the cafeteria's pasty mashed potatoes would stick to a wall for a week. Could the gray hamburgers give cancer to a mouse? And who was getting paid for all the plastic cups of applesauce that no one ever ate?

Someone suggested having a food critic review a cafeteria meal each month.

"The *New York Times* food critic wears disguises at restaurants so they don't know who she is," said Jennifer.

"Cool," said a boy named Sammy. "We have a gorilla suit I could wear. They'd never know it was me."

"Sammy," said Jennifer. "They wear a disguise, like a wig or floppy hat. So no one recognizes they're the world-famous food critic. That way, the restaurant doesn't whip up a great meal for them, while it's feeding the regular customers the usual poison."

Sammy nodded. "So, as soon as the cafeteria ladies saw the gorilla was back, they'd know it was the reviewer from the *Dash* and give me steak and lobster."

"Might be worth it," said a boy.

"We could all dress like gorillas," Sammy said. "Finally get a decent meal."

"I don't know," said another boy. "You really think a gorilla would stick out in the cafeteria?"

Jennifer had another idea, though it sounded way complicated. She'd clipped a brief article from the *Tremble County Citizen-Gazette-Herald-Advertiser* about the county's September zoning board meeting. The zoning board had decided to enforce local law 200-52.7A, which had been on the books since 1924 but had been ignored for years. The story said the law prohibits "accessory structures in the front half of a housing lot." The story said if Tremble was to continue being the richest, tidiest suburb in the Tri-River Region, zoning laws must be strictly obeyed.

Adam nearly slipped into a coma. Had Jennifer lost her mind? A zoning story? "What's the point?" said Adam.

"Well, my dad's a lawyer . . ." she said.

"Please," said Adam. "This is not the Biography Channel."

"Dad says it probably means basketball hoops in driveways and on sidewalks are a zoning violation."

"What?" Adam said.

"They're going to tear down our hoops."

The room got so quiet, you could've heard a basketball swish on the playground three floors below. "Give me that," Adam said. He skimmed the article. "I don't see anything about basketball hoops. . . . Wait . . . are you saying a hoop is a quote-unquote 'accessory structure'? . . . What's the 'front half of a housing lot'?"

"The half near the street," said Jennifer.

At first, Adam hadn't been sure if they needed a second Spotlight Team, then, ten seconds later, he was positive they did. Make a kid get rid of his hoop? Declare it a zoning violation? Tear it down? What was wrong with grownups?

This was what Adam loved most, a juicy outrage to investigate, a story that would put him back on the streets, require him to take death-defying risks to safeguard the common good. He and Jennifer decided to do some research and report back to the staff on how to best handle this travesty of justice.

"All right," said Jennifer. "Now we've got ourselves a story list." She read off ideas and asked for volunteers.

With most kids, it was hard getting them to agree to a single story. But this Phoebe, this pushy third grader, wanted to do every one, and when

15

Adam kept choosing older kids, she jumped out of her seat.

"Hey, it's not fair only middle schoolers get to be on the Spotlight Team," said Phoebe.

"Look," said Adam. "Older kids get first shot. When I was in third grade, I felt honored—I mean honored—if they assigned me a one-paragraph news brief."

"That stinks," squeaked Phoebe.

Adam placed his hands over his head. *Phoebe,* he thought, rhymes with *Totally and Completely Dweebie.* But he didn't say it. He knew if he was going to do this coeditor deal with Jennifer, he had to be what his father called a "constructive force." He decided the easiest thing would be to assign her a story that was too hard and then they'd never see her again. He looked down the list and suggested the Dental Association smile contest at the mall. She'd never pull it off. "Good story," said Adam. "I bet Cable TV Action News 12 will be there."

"Great," squeaked Phoebe. "Can I do Eddie the janitor, too?"

Adam could tell, this Phoebe was one of those young people who could push you to the edge, but all he said was, "We'll see."

16

After the meeting, Adam was chatting with two middle-school boys when he felt a sting at the back of his neck.

"Got to go," said Jennifer, waving her straw. "You know how Mr. Landmass is if we're late for Geography Challenge."

Adam rolled his eyes. "Geography Challenge? Isn't it Quiz Bowl Gladiator Tuesday?"

"That's every other Tuesday and Thursday," said Jennifer.

"I forgot this wasn't the other Tuesday," said Adam. "Aren't we on A schedule today?"

"Close," said Jennifer.

"It's B schedule?" said Adam, banging his palm against his forehead. If they were on B schedule, it meant he had a baritone lesson right after Geography Challenge. He'd just put the horn back in his locker—for nothing. Now he had to go down to the first floor and back up to the third in two minutes, lugging that three-foot-long, ten-pound piece of brass. Right.

Jennifer said, "Thank you, Jennifer. You saved my butt again, Jennifer."

"Yeah," mumbled Adam, "thanks." Jennifer did save him, practically daily. It was embarrassing, and he raced off. At his locker, he twirled the tumbler but was in such a hurry, he messed up his combination and had to do it a second time, then a third. The hallway was emptying, the last kids disappearing into class. He got slowed up again trying to wedge the baritone out of the locker. Adam was sure the person who designed the lockers at Harris Elementary-Middle had played the harmonica.

"Excuse me. Hey, excuse me."

What was that squeaky noise? Adam gave the baritone one last hard tug and it sprang loose, the momentum landing him on the floor.

"Excuse me. Hey, excuse me."

He felt like he was in one of those nervous dreams he'd been having a lot lately, where he kept trying to get to the finish line of a big running-club race, but for some reason he'd veer off the track and could not get back.

He stood up, whirled around, and pinpointed the squeak. Phoebe! Just what he needed, a third grader who didn't know her place.

"Excuse me, but I really wanted to talk to you alone about this Eddie the janitor story," Phoebe squeaked. "I didn't want to say too much at the

18

meeting. Thought we ought to keep it a little hush-hush."

Secret Agent Phoebe, Adam thought. He could already hear Mr. Landmass in Geography Challenge: "Ah, Mr. Canfield, late again. If you can't locate room 328 in a timely fashion, tell me how will you ever locate the Serengeti Plain at the next meet?"

"Look, kid," Adam said to Phoebe. "Do you happen to notice the corridors are empty? Do you happen to notice we're late for eighth period?"

"This is important," said Phoebe. Adam glared at her. He was rushing toward the up stairway, hunched forward, trying to maintain the exact center of gravity needed to balance a full backpack plus an instrument case as big as a bathtub. She would not go away. Finally he stopped.

"What?" he screamed. "What is so important that I'm going to be late for Geography Challenge? Go ahead, Secret Agent Phoebe, you can tell me. I used to be in the FBI myself."

Phoebe ignored his crabbiness. She had three older brothers, so it was normal for her to be hollered at by big boys. She stared right up at Adam. "Eddie the janitor could be really important for us," she

19

said. "Have you seen all those keys on his belt? He can get in anywhere in this building."

"What are you talking about?" said Adam.

"I mean, I think he's more than a pine tree," said Phoebe.

"A pine tree?" said Adam.

"You know," said Phoebe, "a pine tree, a story that's good at any time."

"Evergreen," said Adam. "Evergreen. Not pine tree. Evergreen."

"Whatever," said Phoebe. "The point is, a good story on Eddie might help us—"

"STOP!" Adam yelled. "Are you out of your mind? I'm late for class and you're telling me the guy who empties the wastebaskets is the news scoop of the century?" He bolted off.

But when he'd put a safe distance between them, he turned and shouted, "Do it! I don't care. Do the stupid story! I warn you, though. If it turns out so boring we can't use it, don't come crying to me. . . ."

As he raced around the corner, a piercing sound echoed through those empty halls, a loud, squeaky Phoebe "YES!"

chapter 2

The Bunker

The bell rang to end world history class. Mr. Brooks had just reached the part in *The Story of the Roman Empire* when the great mathematician Archimedes runs through the streets of Syracuse naked. "Sorry, boys and girls," said the teacher, closing the book. "We'll just have to hold on to that thought until tomorrow. You have the reading for tonight. Hurry, young scholars. *Tempus fugit;* time is fleeting. *Ave atque vale!*"

Adam quickly gathered his books and, keeping his head down, tried to slip out unnoticed. He was hoping Mr. Brooks had forgotten that he had been late for class again today. Adam was almost to the door and could see Jennifer waiting for him in the hallway, when the teacher's voice stopped him cold. "Adam Canfield," said Mr. Brooks. "I need a word with you."

The teacher had his grade book open. He placed a sheet of paper under the row of boxes beside Adam's name. "Notice anything?" asked Mr. Brooks.

Over half of Adam's boxes had dots.

"Do you know what those dots are?" asked Mr. Brooks.

Adam was pretty sure he did, but was hoping against hope there was just the teeniest little chance they might be good dots.

"Class participation?" asked Adam.

"Tardiness," said Mr. Brooks. "We're three weeks into the school year, Adam, and you've been late to my class ten times." It was true. Adam's row of boxes looked like it had caught the chicken pox.

He glanced out the door. Jennifer was waving frantically.

"I don't like to make too much of these things," said Mr. Brooks, "especially with a good student, but—is there a problem, Adam?"

Was there a problem? Of course there was a problem. Adam was the most overprogrammed middle-school student in America. He was on the verge of being enriched to death. The whole world plus Adam's parents were yelling at him to hurry up or he'd be late for his next activity. Late for baritone horn lesson, late for jazz band, late for marching band, late for the Math Olympiad club, late for the Quiz Bowl Gladiator meet, late for Geography Challenge, late for soccer, late for swimming, late for snowflake baseball, late for running club, and, yes, late for weekly rehearsals of the Say No to Drugs Community Players. No matter how hard Adam tried to concentrate on where he was supposed to be next, in the end he always seemed to be the late, late Adam Canfield.

And now, because he was getting yelled at by Mr. Brooks — his favorite teacher — for being late to World History, he was going to be late for the principal. Late for his meeting with Mrs. Marris! It was amazing how a few little problems could multiply and destroy a person.

Of course, Adam did not mention any of this to Mr. Brooks; it was way too complicated to explain to a grownup. He just mumbled something about having trouble adjusting to a new school year and promised to try harder.

"Punctuality," said Mr. Brooks. "Very important. From the Latin, *punctum.*" Adam was nodding a lot now, hoping it wasn't too obvious that he was sliding sideways out the door.

"Adam," said Mr. Brooks. "Let's make the effort."

"Yes, Mr. Brooks," Adam said, and unable to restrain himself a second longer, he whizzed off.

The hallway was empty. Jennifer was gone. The bell for the next period was ringing. He raced to the principal's office.

Adam had hoped to sneak into the office unnoticed and then act totally overlooked, perhaps even make it seem that he was a little offended at having been kept waiting for his turn to see the principal. But hurtling down three flights to the main floor, his baritone case clanging against every step, Adam arrived about as unnoticed as the lead fire truck at the Fourth of July parade. Worse yet, he was speeding and took the turn into the office too wide, losing control and ricocheting into the far wall. The baritone case popped open, his music spilled all over the floor, and Adam fell backward, escaping serious injury only because his overstuffed backpack doubled as an air bag.

"Adam Canfield, I presume." It was Mrs. Rose, the school secretary, a stern-looking woman with permed white hair that arched upward for a good nine inches, then formed a neat circle.

The office counter was so high, all Adam could see of Mrs. Rose as he looked up was her perfectly circular head. In the lower grades, there were always rumors about Mrs. Rose having no body, that she was just a permed head placed on the counter by the principal to frighten children.

"You *are* Adam Canfield?" the permed head asked coldly, glancing dramatically at the wall clock. Adam knew what she was thinking: Only a madman or royalty would show up late for Mrs. Marris.

"The principal is waiting," said the permed head, motioning for Adam to follow. A buzzer sounded, freeing a door latch, and Adam stepped behind the counter.

Immediately he noted that the permed head also had legs, long ones. In fact, Mrs. Rose could move them really fast, and he had trouble keeping up as she sped to the next inner office. There, Adam encountered another fearsome grownup, Miss Esther, the principal's personal secretary. Miss Esther was unbelievably old, a very mysterious figure at Harris Elementary-Middle School. No one had a clue what she did besides making announcements over the loudspeaker.

Miss Esther did not look up—a bad sign, Adam thought—and Mrs. Rose did not break stride, leading him through another door and down a flight of steep concrete stairs to a place that few kids had ever seen, but all dreaded.

The Bunker.

Mrs. Marris's office was the school's old civil defense bomb shelter.

It was built long ago, during the 1950s, when Tremble County officials feared the Russians had a nuclear warhead pointed at Harris Elementary-Middle School. The Bunker was an enormous windowless room with an astonishingly long desk. Behind the desk, on the white cinder-block wall, were dozens of photos of Mrs. Marris smiling and posing beside important-looking grownups. Staring at the photos too long could be deadly; Mrs. Marris had the exact same smile in each one, and Adam suddenly felt nauseous from absorbing too big a dose of smiling Marrises.

In a throne-like chair behind the desk sat the actual Mrs. Marris, smiling, of course, and twittering with Jennifer. Adam glanced toward Mrs. Rose for introductions, but she was gone, and it occurred to Adam that with her speed, Mrs. Rose might be a great choice to coach the running club.

"Adam," said the principal, lifting her smile a few notches. "At last we have the honor. Am I right? Does the Bible tell us that Adam was the *first* man?"

Adam knew where this was leading.

"I assume you must be no relation to your biblical namesake," Mrs. Marris continued, "since you are always the *last* Adam. Ha! Ha! Ha!"

Adam sneaked a knowing look at Jennifer.

"DON'T MAKE EYEBALLS AT ME, YOUNG MAN!" Mrs. Marris hollered in a voice so hot and sharp, Adam feared he would melt and drip off the seat. But in an instant, Mrs. Marris was smiling doggedly again. "Jennifer tells me you had your first meeting of the *Dash* yesterday."

Adam nodded. Why had he agreed to be Jennifer's coeditor? At the moment, he blamed her for all his problems.

"Well, good," said Mrs. Marris, smiling. "What I tell new editors each year is that we do our best to run a tight ship here at Harris Elementary-Middle School. And as editors, I would hope you will always ask yourselves, Is this story helping propel the Good Ship *Harris* forward? Because we certainly don't want the kind of stories that poke holes in our bow, so to speak—bad stories, unhelpful stories, *negative* stories."

As Mrs. Marris spoke, Adam and Jennifer smiled and nodded, though they had no clue why. There was something about adults who smiled at Adam while they forced him to do stuff that gave him the creeps. He preferred his mother's method of yelling and telling. At least he knew where he stood.

"The other thing to remember," Mrs. Marris said, "is that the *Dash* is not just any school paper. It is an *award-winning* newspaper, and I expect you to continue that glorious tradition."

Adam understood what she meant. Award certificates and photos were plastered all over the bulletin board in room 306. Every spring for as long as Adam could remember, there was a photograph in the local paper announcing that the *Dash* had again won a prestigious "Citation for Excellence" in the county student-newspaper competition. Each year that photo in the *Tremble County Citizen-Gazette-Herald-Advertiser* looked exactly the same: the *Dash* editors stood in the center holding plaques, flanked by Mrs. Marris and Sumner J. Boland, publisher of the *Citizen-Gazette-Herald-Advertiser.*

And that wasn't all. Every year, the local cable company, Bolandvision Cable, sent a Cable TV Action News 12 crew to do a feature on the *Dash*'s citation for excellence. Adam could not figure out what the fuss was. As far as he could tell, any student paper that filled out an application got one of those annoying citations. Adam had been in 306 when News 12 had arrived last year. The News 12 reporter picked out four kids—one white, one black, one Hispanic, one Asian (two boys, two girls) and had them sit at computers, pretending to write award-winning stories. The News 12 reporter asked just one question—"Is it fun working for the paper?"—then, in the middle of the answer, walked away. When Adam and his parents watched Boland-vision Cable that night, there were a few shots of kids, but mostly it was Mrs. Marris and Sumner J. Boland of Bolandvision Cable talking about how quality education was Tremble's greatest asset.

"Adam?" Mrs. Marris said now, circling out from behind her desk and heading his way. "Adam. Are you with us? I have a wonderful story for the next *Dash* about a kindly woman who has passed on and left a gift to our school." She paused, but when Jennifer and Adam just stared, Mrs. Marris said, "You may want to pull out some paper and take notes." Adam immediately searched his backpack, sifting through textbooks, back issues of *Mad* magazine, his three favorite Calvin and Hobbes books, a bunch of CDs, a couple dozen empty iced-tea cartons, all coated in a thin layer of pistachio nutshells. Privately he gave thanks that this was a rare day when he was able to find a sharpened pencil in there.

The principal explained that not much was known about Miss Minnie Bloch, who had "gone to her reward" a few years back at age ninety-two. She had lived alone, Mrs. Marris said, never married, had no surviving relatives, and was a sweet, warm woman with a fondness for children and animals. She loved Tremble, Mrs. Marris said, and was a life-long resident. The principal explained that Miss Bloch had left money to several groups, including the Tremble animal shelter and Harris Elementary-Middle.

"And then I'd like you to write," Mrs. Marris said, and here she started talking very slowly, "'School officials . . . have decided . . . to spend the money for general improvements . . . according to Miss Bloch's wishes.' All righty? 'General improvements, according to Miss Bloch's wishes.' All righty?" The principal peered over their shoulders at their notes. "All righty, 'general improvements, according to Miss Bloch's wishes.'

"Good," said Mrs. Marris. "Sound like everything?"

It sounded like nothing to Adam—he had a zillion questions—but something about Marris made him feel it would be impolite to ask even one.

"Mrs. Marris," said Jennifer. "Should we say how much money Minnie Bloch left the school?" Adam's eyes popped open and he looked at Jennifer with fresh respect.

31

"Oh, Jennifer, I don't think that's necessary, do you?" said Mrs. Marris. "Everything these days is money, money, money. Who has the most expensive car, the biggest house. Don't you think it's the thought that counts?"

The three smiled and nodded, and then Mrs. Marris said, "I really do feel you have enough for a lovely story," and from her tone it was clear that the interview was over.

"One more thing," said the principal, looking at Jennifer. "You're doing a story on Multicultural Month?"

Adam studied his feet. "That's January," he said. "We thought it could wait awhile." Adam hated Multicultural Month. They never talked about the *real* stuff that went on between different kids at school. Jennifer had told him to ease up, that it was just a harmless way for suburban people to pretend they loved everybody the same, but Adam was not convinced. During Multicultural Month, they spent their time making annoying recipes from other countries, dressing up in native costumes from around the world, and learning to say hello in sixty languages. Last year Adam's teacher made him wear a sheet—

he couldn't remember why, something to do with Italian people.

"I suppose it can wait a month," said Mrs. Marris. "It's just all those wonderful foods and costumes. It's the high point of the year for our students. You looked so cute in your Roman toga last year, *Adamo Canfieldio.*"

"He did, didn't he?" said Jennifer, and Adam took back every nice thought he ever had about Jennifer Brownnose Kissbutt.

"Go now," Mrs. Marris said. "And remember, Adam, what is your job?"

"Coeditor?" he said.

"Propel the Good Ship *Harris* forward," said Mrs. Marris. "Poke no holes in the bow, so to speak."

chapter 3

The Coeditor Blues

Adam's mind was made up. He was turning over a new leaf. From now on, he was going to make daily lists of Things To Do, so he would always know precisely where to be, when. Never again would he get a tardy dot from Mr. Brooks. People were about to witness a new Adam Canfield. Before going to bed now, he wrote down all the important things on his schedule for the next day. It took half an hour; the list came to a little over two feet long. No more rushing around like a chicken with its head cut off.

The New Adam remembered his baritone without Jennifer reminding him. The New Adam remembered this was the second other Thursday of the month, and—miracle of miracles—he was not late for Quiz Bowl Gladiator practice. Jennifer pretended to faint when he walked in on time, but Adam ignored it, not wanting to encourage that kind of humor.

Their coach, the Supreme High Gladiator Chieftain (really just Mrs. Finch, the guidance counselor), began practice by quizzing the young warriors on long lists of facts. The warriors next used the Supreme High Gladiator Chieftain's desk computer to visit the nationally sanctioned Quiz Bowl Gladiator website and sharpen their response times to trivia questions. Each question was assigned a point total, according to degree of difficulty. Jennifer had the highest total among Harris warriors for a five-minute session: 114,712 points. She was the only one at Harris to reach a True Gladiator rating; the best Adam had scored was Gladiator-in-Training.

Afterward, Adam went to soccer practice and Jennifer to tennis, and then the two rode the late bus to Adam's house. Jennifer liked going over to Adam's. Both his parents worked and he was an only child, so there was no one to pester them—like Jennifer's twin third-grade sisters.

35

The coeditors needed to figure out which stories would actually be getting done for the October issue.

Adam's mom had left them a bowl of tuna, baby carrots, and celery sticks in the kitchen refrigerator along with a bag of Cheez Doodles on the kitchen table. Her note said they could each take a soda from the garage refrigerator.

They had lots to do and had planned to work at the computer while they ate. But it was a perfect, balmy fall afternoon, and they couldn't help themselves. For a half-hour, they shot baskets out front on Adam's hoop, a big portable one on the edge of the curb that they shot at from the street. Having someone to play with was a treat, but the thing Adam loved about basketball was that he didn't need anybody. For football he had to have at least one other person for a catch. With baseball, it took a dozen for a decent pickup game. But basketball—he spent hours practicing alone, dribbling without looking at the ball, strengthening his opposite-hand lay-up, making himself better for the day when it counted.

He and Jennifer played one-on-one, horse, knockout, and 5-3-1 before going inside, where they grabbed sodas and the Cheez Doodles, then headed for the family room in the back of the house. Jennifer watched Adam entering each room and jumping as high as he could, trying to touch the top of the door frame or ceiling.

"You know why boys do that?" she asked.

"What?" said Adam.

"Jump when they enter a room."

"No," said Adam. "Why?"

"I don't know," said Jennifer. "That's why I asked."

"Oh," said Adam. "I thought you were giving me a Quiz Bowl Gladiator question. I figured the correct answer was something like 'male frontal lobe hypersynaptic jumping reflex.'"

"That's good," said Jennifer. "Someday you'll be a True Gladiator, too. But I'm serious. Why do boys jump from room to room like that?"

"Never thought of it," said Adam. "I guess it makes me feel taller, reaching things so high up."

"Mom says she can always tell a house with boys from the fingerprints on the ceiling," said Jennifer.

Adam pretended to be offended and rolled his eyes.

"DON'T MAKE EYEBALLS AT ME, YOUNG

MAN!" Jennifer shouted, and they collapsed on the couch, laughing hysterically.

"Is that Marris a lizard or what?" said Adam when he'd finally regained his composure. "It will be a miracle if we can get one interesting fact into this newspaper."

A half-dozen stories had been turned in so far. The kid who did the Halloween safety tips simply rehashed the press release, and Jennifer suggested displaying it in a box, with a check mark for each tip.

The article on the Say No to Drugs Community Players was also dull, a set of dates for tryouts and a list of times when the group would be rehearsing. Jennifer and Adam agreed that was all they needed for now. As the school year cranked up, they'd have to write bigger stories about the Say No's. For reasons that baffled the coeditors, the Say No spring pageant was a huge deal. It got more press than every other activity at Harris combined. Every politician within one hundred miles would squeeze onto the Harris stage to have his picture taken saying no to drugs.

Whatever attracted them, Adam knew it had

nothing to do with the quality of the theatrical production, which was numbingly boring.

Except two years ago. That year Franky Cutty, a very with-it older kid now at the high school, had dressed up as a giant marijuana cigarette. He had totally wrapped himself in white packing paper, spiked his black hair so that it was the only thing that could be seen coming out of the top of the paper, and used dry ice for smoke. All the kindergarten Say No's formed a circle around him onstage and wagged their fingers at Franky the Joint, chanting, "Get Out of Our Town! Get Out of Our Town!" As the curtain fell, the little Say No's chased Franky offstage, wagging their fingers to thunderous applause from the student body. For five minutes, kids in the audience refused to go back to class despite all Mrs. Marris's efforts; they were stamping their feet, wagging their fingers, shouting, "GET OUT OF OUR TOWN! GET OUT OF OUR TOWN!" The scene was such a hit—it cinched Franky Cutty's reputation for life. So last year, as an eighth grader, Franky had offered to dress up as a line of cocaine. He said he would make a gigantic dollar bill out of green poster board, roll it around his body, and pour baby powder over his hair so he looked ready to be

39

snorted. Then Franky said that the kindergarten Say No's would toss a net over him and haul him off to jail, chanting, "THROW AWAY THE KEY! THROW AWAY THE KEY!"

For some reason, Mrs. Marris had nixed that idea.

Those kindergarten Say No's were Adam's idea of great theater, and Franky Cutty was Adam's idea of an impressive human being: daring, funny, living on the edge, and not as overprogrammed as Adam.

Adam suggested they run a short sidebar of Franky recalling his most famous role, to go along with the Say No article, but Jennifer disagreed. "That definitely will NOT propel the Good Ship *Harris* forward," Jennifer said. She said she had no problem with poking holes in the bow so to speak, but felt they needed to pick their battles with Marris carefully.

Jennifer did offer to write up the article on Miss Minnie Bloch, the rich old woman who left the school money.

"No," said Adam. "I don't think we're ready to write that yet. I don't think we know enough."

"Come on," said Jennifer. "This is another one —

we just have to cut our losses. Marris gave us enough for an article."

"That's not it," said Adam. "I felt like—like Marris was covering something up. Didn't you think it was strange the way she kept dictating that sentence about how the money was supposed to be used for *general improvements?* She said *general improvements* a thousand times."

Jennifer nodded. "The thing is," Jennifer said, "everything is so strange about Marris, I don't have a clue what's some big scheme and what's Marris just being her bizarre self."

"This will surprise you," said Adam. "But I have an idea. I have a friend working at the Tremble animal shelter who might have information. An adult. Remember Marris said that the rich lady left money to the school *and* the animal shelter? And the lady loved animals? Well, my friend Danny—he's actually my dad's friend, they went to college together, but he's my friend, too—he knows everybody who loves animals in Tremble. He's a placement specialist. His job is getting families to adopt hard-to-place dogs and cats—nippers, biters, three-legged dogs, cats with glaucoma."

41

"Neat job," said Jennifer.

"It is," said Adam. "Plus Danny's like a kid. He'll come over for dinner, then sit with me at the computer playing Quiz Bowl Gladiator. Or he'll hang out while I do homework. He says he likes seeing what kids are doing—he doesn't have any of his own."

Jennifer didn't answer right away. "I really think it's a mistake wasting too much time on this story," she finally said. "But I'm willing to try this one thing. I would like to meet your friend Danny and see the shelter."

She stood up and began pacing the room. "You know," she continued, "maybe the shelter is the story. . . . Yes! It could make a nice feature article." She could already see the headline: "Has This Man Got a Mutt for You!" Jennifer explained to Adam that she'd been doing a lot of research and had learned it was very important for editors to think in headlines. "I read on the Internet about this very famous editor of a women's magazine who dreams up snappy headlines and then finds reporters to write stories to go under them. Isn't that a neat trick? Adam? . . . Adam? . . . Did you hear what I just said?"

"Some of it," mumbled Adam, who considered

headlines indoor work. For a second he feared Jennifer might throw something large at him, but all she said was that she could go to the shelter on Sunday after church.

"That's great," said Adam. "Sunday's the busiest day for adoptions. You'll see Danny in action. He's amazing when he's up."

Adam was pleased. They'd done a lot. They both agreed it would be best to go slow on the cafeteria investigation. They knew it would be a tough series to get past Marris, and they had to be sure every fact was right. Sammy had smuggled a scoop of mashed potatoes out of the cafeteria and, during recess, tossed it against a wall behind the school. He'd even brought in a camera to document it. A week later, mashed potato residue was still visible. But Adam wasn't sure it proved anything. For all Adam knew, his mom's mashed potatoes — which were a fluffy delight — might stick just as long. He was going to talk to Sammy about setting up a control, comparing the stickability of several mashed potato samples.

The Spotlight Team had also conducted a cafeteria survey, asking students if they had any idea what they were eating. It turned out that one day, 70 percent thought their fish patties were Hamburger Helper. But when Jennifer read the story, she realized the Spotlight Team had talked to only ten kids, and she felt that wasn't enough to be a scientific sampling.

"What else?" asked Adam, who was trying to wedge a Cheez Doodle between his nose and upper lip so it looked like a Cheez Doodle mustache.

"I want you to read this," said Jennifer, handing him a piece of paper with writing that covered every line on both sides. It was Phoebe's story on Eddie the janitor. At the top, she had given it a headline: "A Lot More than a Man with a Wide Broom."

"Is it horrible?" asked Adam.

"Just read it," said Jennifer.

This was Phoebe's story:

> The first time I ever talked to Eddie the janitor was at recess, by the small playground, two years ago, when I was in Mrs. Parada's first grade. I saw two baby birds on the blacktop and thought they were dead; they already had bugs on them. But when I got close, they moved their heads and chirped. I told Mrs. Parada and she

44

said, "We'll call Eddie. He always knows how to handle these things."

Eddie came with a shoebox and soupspoon from the cafeteria. He spooned up the birds and put them in the box. He brushed the bugs off with a toothbrush, kept the babies in his office in the boiler room, fed them with a medicine dropper, and pretty soon they both turned into grown-up mourning doves and are now at the district conservation center.

Eddie told me, "Phoebe, that's a perfect sample of what a good janitor does. Whatever needs doing." When a microphone is squealing at an assembly, they call Eddie. When a student gets stomach flu, they call Eddie. Long ago, in the 1980s, before handicapped ramps were discovered, there was a boy in a wheelchair at Harris, and every day Eddie the janitor carried him piggyback up and down the stairs.

Eddie told me, "Phoebe, janitor's a funny job. You're pretty much invisible until something goes bad." His newest

project is building Mrs. Marris a set of cabinets for an electronic system she's having
installed in the principal's office. He's also
remodeling her bathroom.

Eddie Roosevelt James was born in Mis-
sissippi in the 1940s; he is not sure of the
exact year. He was one of twelve children,
and they grew up poor on a small farm they
did not own. As a teenager, he came up
north by himself, because he thought the
laws would be better for black people. He
got a job chauffeuring Mrs. Frederick Lewis
of 125 Dewey Street in North Tremble.
When she died, he chauffeured Mrs. Alan
Clark of 15 West Constable, also in North
Tremble. When she died, Mrs. Clark's
daughter got him the janitor job.

Eddie told me his prize possessions
are his children. He has one son studying doctoring at Howard University in
Washington, D.C.; a daughter at Tremble
Community College studying to be in the
business world; and another daughter who
just graduated from the state university at

Tremble and plans to be a teacher when she finds a job that suits her right.

Eddie says he loves working at Harris Elementary-Middle. He told me, "Phoebe, there is nothing higher up than education. To me, who is miseducated, coming to work at a school each day and seeing children so busy learning every little fact feels as holy as church on Sunday."

Adam put down the paper and turned away.

"Are you sniffling?" said Jennifer.

"Sinus infection," said Adam.

"Right," said Jennifer. "It's really good, isn't it?"

"It's all right," said Adam.

"I think it's terrific," said Jennifer. "Wait until you hear this. Turns out our little Phoebe's a bit legendary." After Jennifer had read the Eddie story, she asked her twin third-grade sisters if they knew this Phoebe person. They didn't—they had different teachers—but they'd heard about her. When the twins were in first grade, an older boy saw a little girl reading a Boxcar Children book on the school bus. The older boy was reading the Boxcar books, too—in fourth grade. The older boy told his teacher, "There's this girl on my bus, she reads a new Boxcar book every day! She's up to number forty-seven! She must be the smartest kid in first grade!"

That was Phoebe.

"Don't you feel bad now, for giving her such a hard time about that story?" Jennifer asked.

"I don't know," said Adam. "You've got to bring a third grader along slow. I don't care if she's read a thousand Boxcar books. Third graders—it is a scientific fact—their brains are not fully developed yet; their frontal lobes are still like Jell-O. When I came out for the *Dash* in third grade, I felt honored—I mean honored—"

"'If they assigned me a one-paragraph news brief, blah, blah, blah.' You are so full of bull, Adam Canfield," said Jennifer. "I know for a fact, you were the moaningest, most complaining third-grade cub reporter who ever lived."

"So what are we supposed to do?" said Adam. "Turn the *Dash* over to the third-grade Phoebes? You know what a pain in the butt she is."

"Good reporters are," said Jennifer.

"Come on," said Adam. "Am I a pain in the butt?"

"You want to know a secret?" said Jennifer. She

leaned close. Jennifer's head smelled good, a mix of fruity apricot shampoo and sweat. "Don't make eyeballs at me, young man!" she whispered, and once again they collapsed on the sofa.

It had been a long day. The room was getting dark, but neither moved to turn on a light. The only sound in the house was the crunch of Adam eating Cheez Doodles.

"I've been thinking," said Jennifer.

Adam was, too—about how spending a few hours with Jennifer was really not that bad.

"About that smiling contest we assigned Phoebe to do at the mall," said Jennifer.

"No," said Adam.

"No, what?" said Jennifer.

"No, I'm not going to the mall to help her do the story," said Adam.

"How did you know I was going to say that?" asked Jennifer.

Adam shrugged, but lately he felt like they shared the same brain stem. He dropped a half-eaten Cheez Doodle back in the bag. His fingers were stained orange; his stomach felt too full. He burped.

"We can't let her go alone," said Jennifer. "She's in third grade."

"You just told me how she was quote-unquote 'terrific' and quote-unquote 'legendary.'"

"Adam," said Jennifer. "Adam!"

"*Jennifer,*" mimicked Adam. "*Jennifer!*"

"Adam, this isn't like you," said Jennifer. "You're jealous. You are."

"Right," said Adam.

"You knew she couldn't do that story when you gave it to her. You wanted her to fail."

"No way," said Adam.

"Yes, way," said Jennifer.

"If it's such a big deal," said Adam, "why don't you go with her to the mall?"

"I will," said Jennifer. "But I thought it would be nice if you came, too. She could learn so much from a reporter with your experience. The *Dash*'s star journeyman reporter teaching the star cub how it's done."

Adam didn't say anything.

"Oh, come on, just do it," she said, smiling at him.

"Oh no. No," said Adam. "Last time you said that—I wound up being the coeditor."

"And that's such a terrible thing!" said Jennifer. She grabbed the cordless phone and called her parents to come get her. Then she stuffed all her things

50

into her backpack and stomped off. "Jennifer," Adam kept saying as he trailed behind her. "Jennifer. Come on, Jennifer, you know what I mean."

But Jennifer had gone mum.

"Jennifer, at least wait inside until your folks get here," said Adam. But he was alone now, staring at the closed front door.

chapter 4
Herbal Problems

All day Friday, Adam kept waiting for Jennifer to apologize. But every time he tried to catch her eye to let her know that it was OK for her to approach him, so he could forgive her, she immediately looked away, like he was diseased goods. That was the problem with Jennifer—she was such an editor type, she wanted to hold all the little Phoebes' hands and do it all for them. Didn't she understand, the best reporters had to be tough as nails and street savvy? Adam's philosophy when it came to cub reporters was sink or swim—throw them in the pool, give stories to the ones who bobbed up, and fire the ones who drowned.

Adam checked his To Do list and realized that after school he had eighteen free minutes between Math Olympiads and soccer practice. He really was on top of things these days and headed up to 306. Jennifer was going to feel terrible about the way she'd treated him. He was going to do reporting on *her* basketball hoop story. Probably get the whole story reported for *her* with one single phone call. He couldn't wait to see *her* face when she realized he was selflessly doing *her* story without even having to be asked.

Jennifer was going to feel miserable about misjudging him.

Adam dialed the number in the phone book and a crisp voice said, "Tremble County Zoning Board."

Adam explained he had a question about the new accessory structure policy.

"That's Code Enforcement," the crisp voice said. "I'll transfer you." There was quiet, then a dial tone. He'd been cut off. Well, so maybe it would take him two phone calls.

Adam tried again and was cut off—three more times. On the next try, he asked for the direct dial number for Code Enforcement. The crisp voice said, "I'd be glad to connect you immediately."

"Please, NO!" said Adam. "Anything but that. I'll dial it myself."

He did and a woman's voice answered, "Code Enforcement."

"Yes," said Adam. "There was an article in the *Citizen-Gazette-Herald-Advertiser—*"

"Honey," said the woman, "I am so busy, I just don't have the time to do all the reading I should, and I feel terrible about it."

"Hey, that's OK," said Adam.

"No," said the woman. "Reading is so important. I need to do better."

"Don't worry about it," said Adam. "See, the reason I'm calling—"

"Well, you are so sweet," said the woman. "You have just made my day. Thank you for your moral support, honey." And the line went dead.

Adam froze. Had that really just happened? He called back.

"Code Enforcement."

"Yes," said Adam. "I'm the guy who just called, about the article in the *Citizen-Gazette-Herald-Advertiser—*"

"Honey, we get so many calls, it's hard to keep track."

"Remember, we were just talking about the importance of reading?"

"It's possible, honey," said the woman. "It's
been so nice—"

"Wait!" yelled Adam, and he quickly explained
that the story he'd read was about zoning officers
enforcing local law 200-52.7A.

"Now, that does sound like one of ours," said
the woman.

Adam said he had a question about what kind of
structures would be affected. He purposely didn't say
basketball hoops. He wanted to keep it vague. Maybe
Jennifer was wrong, and the last thing he wanted to
do was plant the idea in these guys' heads that they
should be tearing down his basketball hoop.

"Well, now, honey," said the woman. "What
you're asking for is an interpretation of the law. Am
I right?"

Adam said he guessed so.

"I am so sorry, but I am not authorized to do interpretations," she said. "You'll have to speak to the
Herbs, honey."

The herbs? Adam thought. Speak to the herbs?
He'd heard of talking to the animals, but speaking to
the herbs? It did not matter. He was going to keep

this woman on the phone until he got an answer. That's how street-savvy reporters work. He'd show Jennifer.

"Which herbs do I speak to?" asked Adam.

"Green or Black," said the woman.

"I don't know," said Adam. "Green or black herbs? Which is better?"

"You know, I can't answer that, honey," said the woman. "They don't allow me to give out opinions over the phone, but in my opinion the Herbs are pretty much interchangeable."

"OK," said Adam. "Then let me talk to a green herb."

"You mean Herb Green, honey?" said the woman. "He's not here right now."

"Then give me the black herb," said Adam.

"Honey, this is the twenty-first century," said the woman. "A man's race should not enter into it. Herb Black is, just for your information, white. It's Herb Green who is black. No matter. Herb Black and Herb Green are both out. On Tuesdays the Herbs do code enforcement. They're out checking to make sure that backyard fences aren't too high, store signs aren't too wide, additions to homes have all eighteen proper permits . . ."

"I'm so sorry, ma'am," said Adam. "I didn't mean to make a racial—"

"Honey, don't you worry," said the woman. "When it comes to race, none of us is perfect. You just learn from this and go forward."

"Yes, ma'am," said Adam. "Look, is there a chance there'd be someone who could answer a simple question about what an accessory structure is?"

"Oh no," said the woman. "No one can speak for the Herbs."

Adam asked when to call back.

"Hard to say," said the woman. "The Herbs, they work eight to four, but they don't keep a fixed schedule. They're in; they're out. As the Herbs say, code enforcement is not forty hours behind a desk. They're constantly rushing out to investigate fresh zoning violations."

"Could I leave a message?" asked Adam.

"You could," said the woman, "but the Herbs are terrible about returning calls."

"Well, when's good to call back?" asked Adam.

"Best time to get the Herbs is morning," she said, "before they go out."

"About eight o'clock?" Adam asked.

"Normally that would be good," said the woman.

"Problem is, it's my job to answer the phone and I get in at nine."

"So the only time to call," said Adam, "is when no one answers the phone?"

"I didn't say that, honey," the woman said. "The Herbs will pick up when I'm not here, if you catch them in a good mood."

Adam was getting the hang of this. He had a hunch you could never catch the Herbs in a good mood, and said so.

"Oh, you're right about that, honey," said the woman. "Code enforcement is thankless work. People think the law means everybody except them. I'll tell you, the Herbs—the stress—this job has aged those Herbs something terrible. Their nerves are shot, their stomachs ruined. It's made them very bitter Herbs."

"I am so sorry," said Adam.

"Just doing my job, honey," said the woman, and the line went dead.

Adam glanced at his notes. He hadn't written a single complete sentence. He ripped up the paper and tossed it in the wastebasket. What a stupid story. Jennifer had no clue—sure it was easy to think up assignments that sounded great. But doing them? It was the reporter who got stuck with all the dirty work. The thing about Jennifer—she really was a typical editor.

chapter 5

High-Pressure Smiling

Jennifer lay in bed, trying to figure out what she was doing that morning. First she remembered it was a day off because even with her eyelids shut, she could tell there was more sunlight in the room than on a school day, when her dad woke her early. That almost made her open her eyes, until she remembered that the twins would be downstairs already, in control of the TV remote, watching Nick or Animal Planet. Jennifer felt she never got a fair chance to watch her shows. The worst thing was, the twins would hide the remote to spite her and forget where they hid it and Mom would start screaming, "Turn off the TV before I throw it out the window." And then, of course, Jennifer got the blame, because she was "oldest and should know better."

She tried pushing deeper under the covers, then froze. It was Saturday. No school! No church! A wave of joy surged through her and she sat bolt upright.

Until it all came back: she was going to the mall to baby-sit Phoebe for the smile contest story. Instantly, all the juices drained out of her, and Jennifer flopped back on the pillow.

She hated Adam.

The two girls met at 11:30, a half-hour before the contest. Phoebe was standing with her mom, and as Jennifer walked up, she could hear Phoebe hissing, "You can go now, Mom. Really, you can go. Bye, Mom. I mean it."

"Hello, you must be Phoebe's mother," Jennifer said in a reassuring coeditor's voice. Then Jennifer explained that her parents had some shopping to do and would be happy to take the two girls home.

It was easy to see Phoebe had thought of everything. Her hair was in a ponytail with two barrettes on each side so her bangs didn't fall in her eyes when she took notes. She wore pants with a back

61

pocket for a reporter's notebook and kept sliding her hand back there to make sure the notepad hadn't fallen out.

"Got plenty of pens?" asked Jennifer, knowing the answer, but trying to make conversation.

"Right here," said Phoebe, twirling around to show Jennifer her leather backpack. "Eight pens, plus a camera and two extra notebooks."

"Whoa," said Jennifer. "You covering a smile contest or an earthquake?"

"I know what you mean," said Phoebe, "but I was surprised—for the Eddie the janitor story, I filled two reporter's notebooks on both sides. The first time I interviewed Eddie, I was thinking, I'm going to get one page of notes, at most. He kept answering yes, no, yes, no. When I asked him to tell me his life story, he said, 'Young lady, there's not much to tell.'"

"I hate when that happens," said Jennifer.

"That's happened to you?" said Phoebe. "Well, I got double worried, because I'm thinking, What if that guy Adam was right? What if Eddie was a crappy story? So I just started asking everything I could think of: 'How'd you save the baby birds? How'd you know to feed them with the eyedropper? How'd you

62

know about using a toothbrush to wipe off bugs?'
Eddie started talking in sentences and my notebook
started filling up. It was like he got patience for me.
He said, 'You like all those nitty-gritties, don't you,
girl?' And I said, 'You bet, Eddie.'"

"On my fourth visit," continued Phoebe, "Eddie
said—"

"Fourth visit?" said Jennifer.

"Oh yeah," said Phoebe. "The fourth visit was
when he said he was going to have to set up an
office for me in the boiler room. And on the fifth
visit—"

"Fifth visit?" said Jennifer.

"Oh yeah, on the fifth visit, Eddie let me tag
along when he worked in Mrs. Marris's office after
school. That was so neat being in the Bunker when
everyone was gone for the day."

"That is neat," said Jennifer. "Last time I was in
the Bunker, Marris grilled me like a hot dog on
Memorial Day weekend. I was so nervous, I could
barely think."

Phoebe stopped in her tracks. "You get nervous?
The coeditor of the *Dash*? I don't believe it."

"Even the coeditor of the *Dash*," said Jennifer.

"Can I tell you something off the record?"

Phoebe said. "You seem like a nice person for a big kid. But that coeditor Adam guy, I don't think he likes me. Even if I do great on this story, I think he'll say it stinks."

"Oh no," said Jennifer. "Why would you think that?"

"He yelled really loud at me for no good reason."

"He's under a lot of pressure," said Jennifer. "It makes him stupid sometimes. Don't take this wrong, but you're a third grader; it's hard for you to understand. In middle school, they have us so pro-grammed, the pressure builds and builds. You just happened to be in the way when Adam needed to blow. The thing about Adam — he's a great reporter. He cares about truth too much to lie about whether a story's good or not."

"I don't know," said Phoebe. "It seems like he's prejudiced against third graders."

"Nah," said Jennifer. "He used to be a third grader himself."

"Sounds like you like him."

"I'm actually unbelievably pissed at him," said Jennifer. "Last night I told my mom I never wanted to see that jerk again. And Mom said, 'Jen, you must have patience for middle-school boys. They're slow developing.' Mom said they're like cartoons. Funny to watch, zipping around a lot, but inside, there's nothing there yet except the back side of the cartoon."

"We're still off the record?" said Phoebe. "That Adam guy said Cable News 12 might be here. I think maybe he gave me this story because he thought I'd do terrible compared to News 12."

Jennifer just stared at Phoebe. To prepare for being a coeditor, she had read a book over the summer about the ten secrets to becoming a great manager. But there wasn't a single secret in that book that seemed to cover Phoebe. "Does that brain of yours ever rest?" Jennifer said, then smiled kindly. "Look, I guarantee, you will do a better job than News 12."

"I know," Phoebe said. "Why are they so bad?"

"Their news always makes me sleepy," said Jennifer. "A truck crash on the Beltway, a spelling bee champion, a triple murder—every story feels the same."

"Jennifer, you know what I like about you?" said Phoebe. "You give me confidence."

"That's my job," said Jennifer. "It's my job as coeditor to be here for you."

"Is that Adam guy coming, too?" asked Phoebe.

"No," said Jennifer.

"Isn't it his job to be here for me, too?"

"I think he had a, uh, soccer game," said Jennifer.

Phoebe looked at Jennifer funny. "Can I ask you a favor," the third grader said. "Can you not help me on this story?"

"I won't be a bother," Jennifer said. "I just thought, if you had some questions, I'd hang out, and—"

"I need to do it myself," said Phoebe. "I need to show that Adam guy I can do it. Otherwise he'll say you did it all for me."

"He's not like that," said Jennifer.

"I think he is," said Phoebe.

The press release said the contest was being held along the west strollway, in the opening by the Gap. Sure enough, there were sixty folding chairs set up in rows in the middle of the strollway and three tables along the side—one for contestants to sign in, one for judges, and one for the press. As children arrived, they were given a packet that included rules, a toothbrush, dental floss, and a foot-long construction-paper tooth with a number. The paper tooth came with a piece of string and was to be worn around their necks for identification purposes.

The winner would be the child who smiled longest. First prize was a five-hundred-dollar savings bond.

When Phoebe went to the press table, the woman there assumed she was confused. "Oh no, sweetheart," the woman said to Phoebe, "you want the contestants' table. That's for little smilers like you. Hurry, now—get your paper tooth."

Phoebe explained that she was actually a reporter, from the *Dash,* the Harris student newspaper.

"A reporter? Oh, is that adorable," said the woman, calling over her friend Phyllis. "Phyllis, look, she's a reporter. Did you ever see anything so cute in your life? From the Harris *Dash.*"

"The *Dash*?" said the woman named Phyllis. "Where did they ever get a name like that?"

Phoebe was getting irritated. They were wasting time she could be using to do pre-game interviews. "Harris . . . Elementary . . . *DASH*"—and here Phoebe made a dash mark in the air with her finger— "Middle School," said Phoebe, speaking slowly so as not to confuse the poor women.

"And where's the *Dash* photographer?" asked the first woman. "Don't tell me. I bet it's his nap time." After a few more ridiculous jokes, the first woman issued Phoebe a press pass in the shape of a tooth and the Phyllis person pinned it on.

As Phoebe turned to go, someone very large bumped into her, stepped on her foot, then elbowed past her to the press table without apologizing.

"Peter Friendly," the man said in a booming voice to the two women at the press table. "Cable Action News 12."

"My favorite TV news station," the first woman said.

"All the news I ever need," said her friend Phyllis.

"All news, all the time," said Peter Friendly, repeating the station's twenty-four-hour news slogan. He explained that unfortunately he had only a few minutes. "We just heard over the police scanner that a four-hundred-pound man sat on his stepson out in West Tremble. Very nasty domestic dispute. Apparently it was intentional. We must get there ASAP. Could be the lead item at the top of the hour. The guys in the News 12 truck are beaming up our remote transmitter; we'll go live on that one. So we're here on the run. Would you mind if we just have all the kids quickly sit in the chairs with their paper teeth and give us a fast smile, pretending the competition has started?"

"We'll have to ask Dr. Cooper," the first woman said coldly. "He is adamant about sticking to the schedule. He's the incoming president of the Tremble Dental Association. A very civic-minded dentist. He puts his patients' teeth first."

"Right," said Peter Friendly. "How about if we videotaped this Dr. Cooper standing in front of our little smilers? Give the doc some free TV exposure."

"Rules are made to be broken," chirped Phyllis. "By the way, I'm Dr. Cooper's wife, Phyllis Cooper. I'm cochair of today's event. I'd be delighted to get him, Mr. Friendly."

"We'd certainly want Dr. Cooper's charming wife standing up front with him," said Peter Friendly, giving Phyllis a big Friendly wink. "I do appreciate it, Mrs. Cochair."

"All news, all the time," said the dentist's wife, high heels clicking as she hurried to fetch her husband.

Phoebe used the time before the contest to interview kids. A girl wearing Tooth Number 12 said she'd been practicing smiling all week. "My best time was two hours and two minutes," said Tooth Number 12. "I'd watch TV and smile. Do my homework and smile. Catch up with my chat room and smile."

Phoebe noticed Tooth Number 12's left leg was bouncing a mile a minute.

"Nervous?" asked Phoebe, who was writing down Tooth Number 12's comments.

"I am," said Tooth Number 12. "I wish I had something to destroy. I like to rip up stuff when I'm nervous."

A girl sitting nearby, Tooth Number 37, said that she had smiled six straight hours one night last week. When Tooth Number 12 overheard this, the color drained from her face and her nervous leg got bouncier. Tooth Number 12 didn't think it possible, smiling six straight hours. She sure hoped it wasn't possible.

"It's all true," said Tooth Number 37's little brother, Tooth Number 38. "She practiced so much, she was talking in her sleep. She kept saying, 'I won, I won. Bananas, bananas.' My mom took a picture of her sound asleep, smiling."

Phoebe had to stop because Peter Friendly was rounding up kids to pretend the contest was beginning. He hurried them into chairs, making sure there was one white, one black, one Hispanic, and one Asian smiler in the front row. "This isn't real," he told the children. "This is just for TV news." After his crew finished taping Dr. Cooper and the charming Phyllis standing in front of the forty-six smilers, the News 12 crew raced off, bumping into chairs and mall shoppers as they left. When Phoebe last glimpsed Peter Friendly, he was shouting into a cell phone and all three beepers on his belt were buzzing or jingling.

The commotion over, Dr. Cooper thanked them for their patience. In his remarks, which he read from note cards, he explained that the latest research showed there are over half a billion cavities in America. He said that the smile contest was intended to dramatize the need for proper dental care, the first of many outreach programs he planned during his two-year term as dental association president. Brushing was vital, he said, flossing essential, and, of course, regular visits to the dentist. But too often overlooked, he said, was proper diet.

"Our children are junk-food junkies," said Dr. Cooper. "If we don't control our kids' sweets intake, we could be looking at a billion new cavities in twenty years."

Phoebe noticed people's eyes glazing over, but

71

they got focused fast when Dr. Cooper's wife, Phyllis, reviewed the rules for the five-hundred-dollar prize. "For a smile to count," she said, "the top teeth must be exposed. The upper lip must be up. Up, up, up. If your lip drops, you lose, you're out, goodbye. The judges' decision is final." She made everyone do a practice smile. The ten judges inspected the forty-six smiles. Number 15 was grinning. Phyllis explained that grins didn't count; you had to show teeth. She said there would be a five-minute break every ninety minutes.

"OK, ready?" said Phyllis, who was holding a stopwatch. "Three, two, one, SMILE!"

Immediately, forty-six upper lips shot up. It was infectious. Soon the judges and parents were smiling. Phoebe was smiling. Even the busy shoppers passing by and trying to figure out what was going on were smiling.

But as often happens in life, smiling is the most natural thing in the world until a person thinks about it. Phoebe had nearly driven herself crazy one night, lying in bed trying to figure out how she fell asleep, and now she could see that same kind of worry creeping over the faces of the forty-six smilers. For the first time in their lives, they were

100 percent focused on their mouths. It was amazing how sore their cheekbones were, how annoying it was to have a tongue in the middle of the mouth doing nothing. At the twenty-two-minute mark, Phoebe noticed a hissing. She suspected a gas leak, until she realized the hissers were smilers straining to breathe through clenched teeth.

At twenty-four minutes, the first Tooth, Number 17, was yanked by the judges and broke down crying. "That's what worried me," her mother told Phoebe in a post-smile interview. "It's a lot of pressure, and she had no teeth to show. Open your mouth, kitty. Let the reporter see." Number 17 obliged, and where her two front teeth would be someday was a gap.

"The Tooth Faiwy took away my baby teeth," sniffled Number 17, her blond pigtails drooping, "and no one bwought me big teeth yet. I am misweble."

"When they inspected her upper lip," explained the mother, "the judges just got air." She took her daughter's cheeks in her hands and said, "Don't you worry, kitten-witten. We'll walk over to McDonald's, get a Happy Meal, and we'll both feel better."

With the first tooth pulled, the rest felt wobbly, and many fell out. After a while Phoebe could tell when a smile was about to go. The hissing got louder, the top lip wiggled, stiffened, drooped, collapsed. The child would look around to see if anyone noticed—but of course the judges were right there and their decision was final.

The defeated smilers looked grim trudging off. A crestfallen Tooth Number 29 told Phoebe, "I tried resting my top teeth on my bottom lip, but the judges kept giving me warnings. I didn't have the energy to go on."

With just a few minutes to the break, parents of the remaining smilers hurried down the strollway. It seemed an odd time to go shopping, but they were back quickly, clutching paper sacks.

"All right," said Phyllis, staring at the stopwatch. "Three, two, one. Stop smiling. Great job. You should be proud. You are all helping advance modern dentistry. You have five minutes. Nineteen smilers left."

The smilers looked droopy, exhausted. Fortunately, their parents were prepared.

"Take these," Number 12's mom whispered, ripping open a ten-pound, giant economy-size bag of M&M's. "You need to reenergize." The girl put the bag to her mouth and funneled in the M&M's.

Everywhere Phoebe looked, little smilers were munching Sweetarts, Sugar Gushers, Necco Wafers, Skittles, Gummi Bears, Crazy Dips, and Brown Sugar Wallops. To wash it down, they took huge gulps of forty-eight-ounce McDonald's supersize Cokes.

It took a while for Phoebe to understand what she was seeing, but as it sunk in, she could not believe it. Quietly she pulled out her camera and snapped the smilers "reenergizing" for Round Two. No one else seemed to notice. She glanced at Dr. Cooper, the charming Phyllis, and the judges, but they were talking among themselves in tight adult circles, congratulating each other on this wonderful community education event.

As Round Two started, the hissing was louder, the smilers looked bug-eyed, their hands shook, and their feet tapped feverishly.

"Where do they get all the energy?" Phyllis marveled. Phoebe didn't say a word, but she was pretty sure this was what a level-one sugar fit looked like.

Halfway through Round Two, she asked Phyllis for a copy of the list of contestants.

"Now, why would you want that, Miss Cutie-Pie Reporter?" asked Phyllis.

Phoebe explained it was to match each smiler's

tooth number with the name on the list to make sure she spelled everything right.

"Aren't you the little worker bee?" said Phyllis. "I can't wait to see your story in the *Dash*"—and Phyllis made a dramatic dash in the air with her finger. "I will be suggesting to Dr. Cooper that the dental association give an award to the student publication that does the most to promote dental hygiene. And I bet you know who I'm nominating. . . ."

"I guess so, ma'am," said Phoebe, who was staring at the floor. Phoebe felt guilty, a traitor to the cause of modern dentistry and everything the dental association, Dr. Cooper, and Phyllis stood for. Was she the only one who saw it? Had she blown it out of proportion? But, no, the same thing happened during the second break.

It was as if the dental association was promoting Rapid Tooth Decay Week, the way the eight remaining smilers wolfed down red licorice, bite-size Milky Ways, Reese's peanut butter cups, creamy caramels, Hershey's Kisses, and Triple-Strength Sugar Booger Dips. "I need another hit from the two-liter!" bellowed Tooth Number 12, taking several mammoth sucks of orange soda.

Meanwhile, over at the press table, Dr. Cooper and Phyllis were busy with the reporter from the *Citizen-Gazette-Herald-Advertiser,* who had finally arrived and was making a note about the need for Americans to change their eating habits.

It took four hours and three minutes, but finally, the winning tooth was crowned, none other than Tooth Number 12. The gentleman from the *Citizen-Gazette-Herald-Advertiser* took a photo of the winner flanked by Dr. Cooper and his cochair, Phyllis.

Everyone crowded around Number 12 and said how great she'd done. The man from the *Citizen-Gazette-Herald-Advertiser* asked if it was fun winning five hundred dollars just for smiling.

"Kind of hard," said Tooth Number 12.

"That's nice," said the *Citizen-Gazette-Herald-Advertiser* reporter.

Phoebe waited for people to leave before asking a few last questions. She didn't want to raise any suspicions.

"I don't know how you did it," said Phoebe. "I never could have lasted."

"I know," said Number 12. "It was hard."

Phoebe asked if anything besides practice smiling had contributed to the victory.

"Well, I'm a cheerleader," said Number 12. "So I'm used to smiling even in the face of defeat."

"Did the M&M's help?" asked Phoebe.

"Huge," said Number 12. "Heading into the first break, I didn't think I'd be able to go on. I kept remembering the girl who said she smiled for six hours. I started dreaming about being home, watching my collection of MTV spring break videos. And then my mom poured those M&M's down my throat. Yipes! My toes were tingling; I could feel my heart pounding. I was riding a sugar wave to victory."

Phoebe took down the quote and closed her notebook. "I think that'll do it," Phoebe said. "Congratulations."

"Yeah," said Number 12. "I'm not smiling for a week, even if it's something funny."

Phoebe reopened her notebook to write that down, then put her pen and pad away in her backpack.

She glanced around. The dental association officials were gone now. A mall custodian was stacking folding chairs on a dolly. Then she spied Jennifer, leaning against the wall, just beyond Bed, Bath &

Beyond. Phoebe walked toward her. It felt good to get away from all those dentist people. She never realized it was so much pressure being around people when you might have to write bad stuff about them. Part of her felt she was a wicked sneak.

"Phoebe," said Jennifer. "How'd it go? A long Saturday afternoon."

"OK," said Phoebe quietly. "Different from what I expected."

"Different?" said Jennifer.

"Yeah," said Phoebe. "It's hard to explain."

Jennifer nodded, then asked, "You get some good shots of the M&M queen?"

Phoebe stopped walking and looked up at Jennifer. "How'd you know?"

"Wild guess," said Jennifer.

"You think it's OK to put that stuff in the story?" asked Phoebe.

"I do," said Jennifer.

chapter 6

"Has This Man Got a Mutt for You!"

Sunday was colder, a blustery autumn day. It would be tough bicycling into the wind. Adam e-mailed Jennifer to see if she still wanted to go. He wasn't sure if she was still mad at him. Jennifer could nurse a grudge pretty good. But the instant message she sent back seemed normal. They were sticking to the plan. After church, she would meet him at the Pancake House by the train station for a late breakfast. Then they would bike to the animal shelter to see Danny.

On the way over, there were a couple of neat

curbs for doing wheelies and grinds, and Adam arrived at the Pancake House twenty minutes late, which was about what Jennifer had expected. She already was sitting in a booth—they loved getting a booth—sipping hot chocolate and leafing through old J. Crew catalogs.

"Heavy reading?" asked Adam.

"Get lost on the way over?" asked Jennifer. She stared at him. He was such a space cadet. "You can take off your bike helmet now," she said. "The ceiling looks pretty safe in here."

"Oh . . . right," said Adam, unbuckling the chin strap and placing his helmet on the booth seat. He ordered blueberry pancakes and a hot chocolate with whipped cream.

Jennifer cut her pancakes neatly into little pieces. Not Adam. First he ate all the whipped cream off his hot chocolate. Then he picked up the top pancake with his hands, turned it over so he could see where the blueberries were, and began eating, making sure every bite had at least one blueberry.

Jennifer didn't seem angry anymore, so Adam didn't see any point in revisiting ancient history. "How'd the smile contest go?" he asked.

"I guess if you wanted to know, you would have been there," said Jennifer, not even bothering to look up from her pancakes.

Adam felt like Jennifer had just kicked a forty-five-yard field goal straight into his stomach. "Look," he said, "I'm sorry you're still angry. I didn't want you—"

"Stop," said Jennifer. "It's over. I've been thinking. This is partly my fault. I did sort of pressure you into being coeditor. You don't have to do it. Honest. I can find someone else. I think Sammy could probably—"

"Sammy?" said Adam. "Sammy can't even do that cafeteria investigation without messing up."

"Well, then, maybe Donald," said Jennifer.

"Donald?" said Adam. "Donald didn't even come to the first meeting."

"Not your problem," said Jennifer. "I'll handle it. There's Robert. Or Franklin . . ."

"I'll do it," said Adam. "I said I would, and I will."

"Don't do me any favors," said Jennifer. "I don't need—"

"Jennifer, stop, stop, stop. I want to do it. I do. I promise."

"You're sure?"

Adam nodded.

"All right," said Jennifer. "Fine. Then I expect you to make things right with Phoebe. The *Dash* needs her, and she thinks you hate her."

Adam rolled his eyes. "I wonder why she thinks that," he said.

"I wonder," said Jennifer.

"How'd she do on the smile contest?" asked Adam.

"I don't know how it'll turn out," Jennifer said. "But I do know this—she worked really, really hard."

The waitress asked if there would be anything else and Jennifer said, "Just the check."

"Wait," said Adam. "An order of mashed potatoes to go."

The waitress looked at him funny and Jennifer said, "You're still hungry?"

Adam leaned toward Jennifer and whispered, "For Sammy. The cafeteria Spotlight Team stickability test."

"Right," said Jennifer, and turning to the waitress, she said, "Definitely mashed potatoes."

"Definitely mashed potatoes it is," said the waitress.

"You got to admit," said Adam on the way out, "I'm thinking like a coeditor."

"You left your helmet in the booth," said Jennifer.

At the shelter, they locked their bikes out front, then raced up the handicapped ramp, which zigzagged twice and was more fun than stairs. The lobby featured a bronze statue of a boy and a girl hugging a dog with the words, *Man's Best Friend.* Nearby was the reception desk. Adam told the woman they wanted to see Danny.

"He expecting you?" she asked.

"We're friends," said Adam.

"Then you're a lucky boy," said the receptionist. "When he's up, Danny's the best." She paged him over the loudspeaker.

While they waited, Adam and Jennifer scanned the forms people filled out to adopt a pet. There were lots of personal questions.

They watched the shelter workers, dressed in dark green polo shirts, rushing through the lobby. Everyone seemed so busy. It looked like a fun place to work.

Pretty soon there was a commotion on the far

side of the lobby. They could hear barking and howling from behind the wall, a door swung open, and a
large, bald man was walking briskly toward them.
"Is my vision deceiving me?" the man bellowed,
cupping his hands around his eyes like binoculars.
"Is that him in the flesh and blood? Adam Canfield,
star of stage and screen, and my former good friend?
The one who's always too busy to visit, yet sends
me e-mails by the thousands?"

Adam smiled shyly, but before he could think of
anything to say, Danny swooped over, lifted Adam,
and gave him a huge bear hug. Adam weighed all of
eighty-five pounds and was barely visible wrapped
inside of Danny's hug. It felt good to Adam, like all
the shyness was being squeezed out of him.

"How you doing, Danny," Adam said after he
was placed back on the ground.

"Boy, you're getting big," said Danny. "Pretty
soon I'll need a front-end loader to lift you. And who
is this—don't tell me, you got married since I last
saw you. And what a beauty. You must have lied
big-time to get her to marry the likes of you."

"This is Jennifer," said Adam.

"*The* Jennifer?" asked Danny. "True Gladiator
Jennifer? At last we meet." Danny bowed. "Jennifer,

explain one thing," he said. "Why on earth would you marry a guy who can't get past Gladiator-in-Training?"

"Brains aren't everything," said Jennifer. "The boy has a good heart."

"That he does," said Danny. "I can see you are an astute observer of human nature, which will serve you well here at the Tremble animal shelter." He motioned for them to follow and headed back through the far door, into an airy, high-ceilinged room full of chainlink cages holding row after row of dogs and cats. As Danny passed, one animal after another came to life, standing on hind legs, barking and meowing as if paying tribute to the master.

"It's like they know you," said Jennifer.

"They do," said Danny. "And I know them. They all want to be fixed up with someone. They have good reason to suck up to me."

Danny explained that Tremble was different from most shelters. Dogs and cats were not put to death. They stayed until a home was found for them. "That's where I come in," he said. "Top specialist in placing the hardest of the hard."

He needed to do a few more placements before he could sit and talk. "I try to do twenty-five before break," he said. "I don't have to; it's just a personal goal." He said they could hang out in the cage room or follow him into the central adoption arena and watch him do matches.

Jennifer was making all kinds of *oohs* and *aahs* and stopping at every cage, but Adam tugged her sleeve. "You've got to see Danny in action," he said. "A wizard."

Before Danny could get to his next placement, two coworkers in green shirts rushed up, nearly trampling Adam and Jennifer. "I need advice, Danny," said the first. "I have a seventy-five-year-old woman who wants to adopt a six-week-old puppy. For a puppy, this is a mangy mutt, so it would be great to find a home. But I'm afraid I can't do it. You know the rules."

The rules said a puppy shouldn't be matched with an old person, because in a few years the result could be a deceased old person and an orphaned dog right back at the shelter.

"Let me see the woman's application," said Danny. "A nonsmoker," he murmured. "Had a dog for a long time that recently died. . . . Lots of activities and clubs. . . ." He looked up from the paper. "Uh-huh," he said, lifting his eyebrows.

"What?" said the coworker.

"Uh-huh," said Danny.

"What?" said Adam and Jennifer.

"Bring me to meet this woman now!" bellowed Danny. She was in a far corner, on the floor, playing with the puppy. When the coworker introduced Danny, the woman jumped to her feet. As they talked, Danny dropped her application on the floor.

She bent right over and picked it up.

"Thanks so much," said Danny. "Would you excuse us?"

He took the coworker aside and said, "Do it."

"But the puppy rule?"

"Made to be broken in this case," said Danny. "Old people are changing their habits — they don't smoke; they join walking clubs; they live salt-free lives. Now, if this woman came in wheezing and spitting blood, it would be different. But, hey — she looks like she can run a four-minute mile. You see her scoop up that application?"

"One more," said the second coworker. "I have a woman looking for a surprise birthday gift for her sister-in-law."

"Stop," said Danny. "Cannot do. We need to see this sister-in-law in person. We don't know what we're dealing with here. There are a million kinds of sisters-in-law."

A small, slight, middle-aged woman was waiting. Danny apologized for the delay, then took her application and read quickly. "I see you live alone," he said. "No children or pets . . . Personal traits? Ah, you're a 'neatnik.'

"OK," he said. "I know a perfect dog." He disappeared into the cage room and, to Adam's amazement, was back in a minute with a match, a miniature mixed breed no more than a foot long.

"Oh, he's precious," said the woman.

"And not a shedder," said Danny.

"You read my mind," said the woman.

"Always," said Danny. "Let me go on. I'm not going to pretend that everything has been peaches and cream for our little friend here. His previous placement did not work. That family had a cat. The cat was as big as our little friend. That family had a couple of young kids. What do kids do best? Grow. A big cat. Two kids getting taller by the minute. What does that do to our little friend? Every morning he wakes up feeling smaller." At this point Danny knelt down, rolled the dog on his back, and scratched his belly. The way that dog was panting and his eyes were shining made Adam wish someone would roll him over and scratch his belly.

"What a silly little precious," said the woman.

"Exactly," said Danny. "Let me go on. What happens when you make a little dog feel small? I've seen it a million times. He's going to prove he's not so small after all. He's going to take all that pent-up resentment and exact his revenge."

"Oh my," said the woman. "What did he do?"

"Chewed up four hundred dollars worth of shoes," said Danny.

"Oh my," said the woman. "I can't have that."

"You won't," said Danny. "If—and this is the big if—you can make this little dog feel big. It's not hard. Just takes imagination. You go to a toy store, buy a couple of—what are they—Teeny Babies?"

"I don't know," said the woman.

"Beanie Babies," said Jennifer.

"A True Gladiator," said Danny. "Exactly. You get a few stuffed cats, a couple little Beanie dogs, leave them around, and suddenly our friend feels large. Every morning he wakes up, he's still bigger than they are. For all he knows, he's a Great Dane. I notice from your form, you have a small backyard—

just one more thing that's going to make him feel big. He'll find a corner—"

"There's a juniper bush," said the woman.

"Perfect," said Danny. "To him, it's going to look like a redwood. His redwood."

"There's a sunken terrace," said the woman, "just a few steps down."

"Perfect," said Danny. "To our little friend it's the Grand Canyon National Park, and he's head ranger."

"Perfect," said the woman.

"Perfect," said Danny.

"Perfect," said Jennifer. Adam was pleased. Jennifer really got Danny.

Danny led them to the employee canteen, a good-size windowless room with food and beverage machines, plus a bunch of tables and colorful plastic chairs. At many tables, men and women in their green shirts sat alone, eating a sack lunch and reading.

"That last adoption," said Danny. "Great one for me mentally." He bought himself an iced tea and peanut butter crackers. Adam and Jennifer didn't want anything. "We just ate," said Adam.

"That's what's great about kids," said Danny. "You think you're only supposed to eat when you're hungry."

"We went to the Pancake House," said Adam.

Danny looked at Jennifer and said, "So you've seen Mr. Manners in action. He still eating pancakes with his hands?"

"Wait," said Adam. "Not fair. Who taught me that? Who said, 'It's the only way to guarantee a blueberry in every bite'? And that is a quote."

"All right," said Danny. "I didn't say it was bad. Just unconventional. It really is great seeing you, kid. You look terrific. They still keeping you busy?"

"To the max," said Adam. "Actually, that's not true. I've got twenty minutes free on Friday afternoons."

"Been out skipping lately?" asked Danny. "We got to go for a big skip. This is the time to do it. I love the river in fall." When Adam was younger, a few times a year, he and Danny would spend an hour or two by the river skipping rocks and talking.

Adam shook his head. "No time," he said.

"I don't know how you guys do it," said Danny. "I wasn't as busy in college as you are in middle school. It is amazing the way they have speeded up the world for you guys. They giving the SATs in pre-K yet?"

"Soon," said Adam. "The smartest kids in our school take it quote-unquote 'just for fun' in seventh grade."

"Sounds like great fun," said Danny. "You know, I didn't play basketball on a team until seventh grade. I just hung at the courts and shot hoops. When did you start club basketball, second grade?" Adam nodded and so did Jennifer.

"And the weirdest thing," continued Danny, "is I don't think you're going to be any better or any smarter than we were. You're just working harder sooner."

"Tell Jennifer your theory," said Adam.

Danny gave him a blank look. "My theory? Which one?" he asked. "There are a million, none worth a cent."

"About history going back and forth," said Adam.

"Oh." Danny nodded. "Not my theory. Hegel's. German philosopher. In every historical period, people behave a certain way, and in the next period, people react to that and behave differently. For every action, there's a reaction. So right now we're in what

I call the Free Market Era of Competition to the Max. Parents and teachers and businesspeople and politicians are so worried that you kids are going to fall behind the kids in the next suburb, they're adding more stuff for you to do so they can convince themselves they're being tougher than ever and you're doing better than ever. And in the next town, they're adding on even more stuff to stay ahead of you. And by the time you guys get to college, you will be so overprogrammed, so drained and pooped and starved for oxygen, it will be just like the 1970s—you'll throw up your hands and scream, 'Enough!'"

Adam and Jennifer were quiet. They were trying to envision a slower future. It didn't seem possible and Adam gave up. He couldn't envision dinner, let alone how the world would look when he was in college.

"Was life better back then?" asked Jennifer.

Danny shrugged. "Every time has its good and bad," he said. "I think maybe it was a little less cutthroat; people might have been a little nicer to each other, more people stopping to smell the roses."

"That's nice," said Jennifer. "What's bad about that?"

Danny got quiet. "Some of the drug stuff," he said. "A lot of good people got deep into drugs in the '70s and never made it back."

Adam felt uncomfortable that the conversation was turning so serious, and Danny must have sensed it, because he leaned over and tried to bite Adam's nose. "Hey, you know who I am?" said Danny. "Mr. Number-One Expert on Nothing. I look back at photos from the '70s — the bell-bottoms, the flower shirts. We looked like idiots."

"Hair was pretty weird, too," said Adam, perking up. "You ever see old film clips of NBA players in their Afro puffs? And the white guys with sideburns to their shoulders? I can't believe how tiny the basketball shorts used to be."

"Someday," said Danny, "you won't believe how long and baggy they are now."

Danny ate a cracker and swigged his iced tea.

"We need information," said Adam. They told Danny about the article they were working on for the *Dash,* about the old woman who died and left the school money. They explained they didn't know much about her and figured Danny might since she'd left money to the animal shelter, too.

"Her name was Miss Bloch, Miss Minnie Bloch," said Adam. "Mrs. Marris told us she was a big animal lover. Figured you had to know her."

"Ruth Ellen Marris told you that old woman loved animals?" asked Danny. "I have known your principal since she was a mouthy twerp one thousand years ago in third grade, and I can tell you, she was a wealth of misinformation back then, too. That is a lie. Poor old Miss Bloch, she hated animals. Or at least was scared to death of them."

The young reporters look puzzled. "Then why would she leave money to the animal shelter?" asked Jennifer.

"I guess because we were nice when she called; we'd always go out to see what her problem was," said Danny. "Usually she'd be reporting some stray dog running around the neighborhood. Some poor mutt looked dangerous to her, and she'd want us to pick it up. And mostly we did."

Adam asked what Danny knew about her. "Not much," he said. "Never met her. She never came to the shelter. Just talked to her on the phone."

"But she was rich?" said Jennifer.

"Well, I gather she left the shelter a nice chunk

of change," said Danny. "I understand we're going to use it to build a volunteers' lounge, for people who donate their time here. But you know what's funny? If she was rich, she didn't have a fancy address. She lived in the Willows. I sent shelter workers there so often, I'll never forget—48 Grand Street in the Willows. You know the Willows?"

They didn't.

"Now there's something that's wrong with schools today," said Danny. "They don't teach you guys any local history."

"Not true," said Jennifer. "We studied all about the five Iroquois nations and how they controlled the whole eastern part of North America and—"

"Right, right," said Danny. "But let me ask you this, and I don't mean any offense to Indians. You got a lot of Iroquois buddies? No? You got any idea how Tremble got to be the way it is today? Where the rich people came from and the poor people and why they brought the railroad out here—you know any of that stuff?"

They didn't.

"You're going to write a story about someone from the Willows, you ought to know these things," said Danny. "I think I still have the special issue of the newspaper from Tremble's seventy-fifth anniversary celebration. You know, we actually had a decent local paper back then—that was something good about the '70s. My memory is, there was a whole article on the Willows. You guys ride right by it all the time—you just never notice. It's the neighborhood behind SuperX Mega Drugs. A bunch of small rundown houses, by the marsh, not far from the sewage plant. Mostly shotgun houses. You could stand at the front door, fire a shotgun, and the bullet would go straight down the hallway and out the back door. Definitely not mansions."

Danny stood, ready to get back to adoptions. "I think you're on to something," he said, tossing the plastic tea bottle into a recycling bin, then making the signal for a two-point field goal. "It didn't figure, how a woman in the Willows had all that money to leave to good causes."

That night for dinner, Adam's mother made his favorite—herb-spiced chicken cutlets with mashed potatoes and peas. It softened the bad feeling Sunday nights had for Adam. Five straight days of school staring him in the face. And a ton of home-work, which he'd left to the last minute, of course.

After dinner he leaped up to clear the plates, spurring his mother to make several sarcastic comments about all the things she never thought she'd see in her lifetime. In the kitchen, alone, Adam grabbed a mound of leftover mashed potatoes and stuffed it into a Ziploc bag for Sammy.

By the time his schoolwork was done, it was past eleven. The New Adam was too tired to write a To Do list, and the moment his head hit the pillow, he was gone. It was not a restful sleep; he did not have pleasant dreams.

Adam is winning his running club race, moving effortlessly into the wind. The track is straight, flat, and clear, but suddenly he takes a crazy turn and is running through a field behind houses and through a vegetable garden. Why did he do that? Some old woman is moaning, "Get out of my garden, honey," and Adam runs faster, but his feet are like lead, and when he looks down, there's a tiny dog locked on his ankle. The faster he runs, the more he gets tangled in the garden's strongly scented, green bushy plants, which, come to think of it, smell a lot like his mother's herb-spiced chicken.

Herbs! Adam woke Monday morning and immediately thought, Herbs! It was early, but he rushed to get dressed, then put his backpack and baritone by the front door. He had ten minutes until the bus. Even his father noticed. "What do we have here?" he asked. "A reconfigured, punctual version of the standard-issue Adam?"

"Yeah, right, Dad," said Adam. "Very funny, Dad." He hurried to the family room and dialed Code Enforcement. It was his fourth try in a week. Adam had decided he would keep calling until he got a Herb on the phone to ask about the hoops. It was a little before eight.

The phone rang three times, then a man's voice said, "Yeah?"

Adam was excited and scared. A Herb! "Is this Code Enforcement?" Adam asked.

"Might be," said the man.

"I'd like to speak to one of the Herbs," said Adam.

"Which one?" asked the man.

"I don't think it matters," said Adam.

"Oh, let me guess," said the man. "I bet they told you the Herbs are interchangeable. Right? Well, I'm going to let you in on something, buddy. Those Herbs may seem like cold-hearted robots to you,

Herb and Herb, the evil Code Enforcement twins, but I know for a fact, each Herb has his own feelings, his own worries, and his own dreams, too."

"I didn't mean . . ." Adam stammered. "I just wanted—"

"The Herbs aren't available," said the man. "Call back at nine, when the receptionist is in." There was a loud click and the line went dead.

chapter 7

A Bad Feeling

Mr. Brooks was a mythic figure at Harris, old-fashioned and proud of it. He wore a bow tie and suit every day and kept his coat buttoned. He was adamant about his disdain for TV, MTV, DVDs, electric toothbrushes, and—more than all his other adamant disdains—cell phones, which he called the rudest development civilization has known since the whoopee cushion.

He so fascinated his students, they devoured any personal fact that he dropped in conversation. Adam knew his favorite teacher was a lifelong bachelor, loved the black-and-white pastries at Blotnick's Bakery, and drove only Chevrolets.

The man kept a jar of hard candies on his desk, and when students answered a tough question, he'd shout, "Gigantic conceptual leap," then toss them a sweet. He had a great arm, and Adam had heard kids say he used to play minor league baseball.

Adding to this aura was his mastery of a dead language, Latin. He told Adam's class that they were on a quest for *veritas.* Truth. When explaining where Virgil ranked among poets, he said *"Virgil est Deus."* Virgil is God. At the end of the period, he did not say, "See you tomorrow"; he said, *"Ave atque vale."* Hail and farewell.

"I won't ask anything of you I don't ask of myself," Mr. Brooks told them. Unfortunately, he asked everything of himself. He explained that history came from many sources, and one source they would use for the founding of Roman civilization was the *Aeneid,* a two-thousand-year-old poem by Virgil. Then he added, "I, of course, have memorized all ninety-eight hundred lines in Latin but won't expect you to—not this year." Mr. Brooks had a gift for making even an ancient figure like Archimedes seem like someone Adam had met.

Mr. Brooks did not have discipline problems; he actually bragged about never giving detentions. By now, Adam would have had a thick stack from anyone else for all his tardies. But Mr. Brooks treated them like grownups. After their talk, Adam felt too embarrassed to be late—at least for Mr. Brooks. On some level, they sensed that Mr. Brooks worshiped knowledge and any disruption would unfairly delay the quest.

It made a big impression on Adam that even hip high-school kids like Franky Cutty idolized Mr. Brooks. A few years before, near the end of school, Franky and some buddies had sneaked into Mr. Brooks's room early one morning and hung a banner across the chalkboard that read *Brooks est Deus!* Brooks is God! When Mr. Brooks saw it, he said that they all should be expelled for "impinging upon my terra firma." He stepped outside, closed the door, and they could hear him blow his nose. When he returned, he said, "Obviously, I'm quite moved," then got on with the lesson.

One of the things that made Mr. Brooks's class so beloved was the board game World Domination, which he played the second half of the year. It normally went on for a month, and one year it lasted six weeks.

Adam had been hearing about it for so long, he already knew the rules. Each student picked the name of a country out of a hat. Each country was worth a certain amount of points depending on how rich and powerful that country is in real life. So the kid who picked the United States had lots of points assigned for food, manufactured goods, military power, and a large, well-educated population. The kid who picked a poor, weak country like Bangladesh got very few points because food was scarce, there were few natural resources, and little military power.

The idea was for each student to improve his country's situation in the world—to raise its point total. What made the game surprising was that the student who got Bangladesh could win if he raised his total by a higher percentage than any other player.

Kids earned extra points by joining with another country to plant more food or build factories. They also could get extra points by going to war, conquering a country, and taking over its points.

Some years Mr. Brooks's class spent the entire month fighting wars. A few years students scored points by forming alliances and forging world peace.

Once—the year Mr. Brooks let the game go six weeks—they founded a world government.

Most years were a chaotic mix of war and peace.

The idea was for students to understand what motivates a country to behave the way it does on the global stage.

At each step Mr. Brooks taught real-life world-history tales that mirrored decisions being made in the game.

When Franky Cutty, who was Iraq his year, got tired of slowly building his manufacturing points, he eyeballed his neighbor, Kuwait. Franky realized Kuwait had a ton of wealth points for oil and few military points. Since it was right next door, Franky saw he could attack and use almost no transportation points. It looked like easy pickings. But then Mr. Brooks had them read about the 1991 Gulf War. Suddenly, the girl who was Kuwait realized she could ally herself with the United States, which would be glad to offer a few of its military points to defend Kuwait in exchange for some of Kuwait's oil points. Within days, Franky Cutty was crushed.

So legendary was World Domination that Adam's class began pestering Mr. Brooks on the first day of school. "When do we start?" they asked. "If we get a bad country, can we trade?" Like any great teacher, Mr. Brooks milked it. He said the game was a reward for working hard. He warned that if they did not meet his standards, they could be his first class not to play.

But as the weeks passed, Adam sensed something was wrong. Mr. Brooks's answers were vague, curt. On this gray Monday, when Adam again prodded him, all Mr. Brooks said was, "Let's not discuss it now." No jokes. No Latin quotations. No peeks at the eight-foot-long game board, the way he'd done for other classes. It gave Adam a bad feeling.

At lunch Adam remembered he had the mashed potatoes in his backpack. They were squished, but not too bad, and after brushing off the pistachio shells, he handed over the samples to Sammy.

He needed to speak to Phoebe—he'd promised Jennifer—but everyone was kept so busy, it was hard getting hold of kids in other grades. Of course, Adam hadn't planned ahead, but Jennifer did. She gave each of her twin sisters an identical note telling Phoebe that the *Dash* coeditors needed to talk to her. Jennifer hoped if she gave it to both twins, one might actually remember to hand it to Phoebe. The note said to be in 306 at 4 P.M.

That afternoon every grade at Harris had its first before-school/after-school voluntary/mandatory class of the year. This was a new prep course for the state tests that the Tremble County School Board had approved the past spring.

Adam naturally had misplaced the room number for his class. He thought it was 224, but when he rushed in, he realized he'd messed up. It was a voluntary/mandatory for second graders.

"May I help you?" asked the teacher. Adam explained he'd confused the rooms.

"What's your last name start with?" asked the teacher. She checked her computer printout. "C? And you're a middle schooler? Room 242."

Adam started to leave, but the teacher said, "Wait. You're supposed to be in 242 and you came to 224? You've transposed your numbers. This is exactly what Mrs. Marris has us on the lookout for. You may be suffering a severe learning disability. This is wonderful. Number transposition is classic. I need your name for a screening referral—"

"I really don't think that's necessary," said Adam. "I'm just a little disorganized." Why hadn't he made his To Do list?

"Learning disabilities can be subtle," said the teacher. "Mrs. Marris is going to be thrilled with me for finding you. With the right help, you could learn to overcome your disability by the time the state test is given in the spring. Or if you're too bad, you might qualify for a special education waiver, a 504 accommodation. You get extra time to take the test. If you're messed up enough, they might give you a week, maybe two weeks to answer each question. An aide could read you the reading comprehension section out loud. Wouldn't that be grand? Who needs a low score? Not you, not Harris, and certainly not the district. I need your name and home-base teacher."

Adam hated himself for what he was about to do. It embarrassed him for people to know. But this teacher was backing him into a corner. He had a feeling if he didn't stop her now, if somehow this woman got his name on that paper she was waving at him, it could take weeks, maybe months, to undo the damage. There was no way out.

Adam whispered, "I'm a four-pluser."

The teacher immediately stopped writing and actually looked at him. "A four-pluser?" she said. "Really? Good for you. Good for us! What's your name again?"

"Canfield," Adam said.

"Canfield?" she said. "Now I remember seeing it." Each year the *Citizen-Gazette-Herald-Advertiser* printed results of the state competency tests for every school in the Tri-River Region. The paper listed the percentage of students in each grade at Harris who passed, scoring three or four. And the percent who failed, the incompetents, who scored one or two. But then, in a special box headlined "Tremble's Best and Brightest," the paper printed names of students who had tallied a perfect score, a four-plus. In all Tremble there were just four four-plusers.

"This won't be necessary," said the teacher, ripping up the referral. "But we can't be too careful, can we?"

Adam thanked her profusely and sprinted to 242. Heaven knows what they would do to him for being late. Or whether they could do anything. According to a note school officials sent home, these sessions weren't technically mandatory. In fact, they couldn't be mandatory; state law limited the mandatory school day to six hours. Rather, the note said, since "everyone's property values depended on the highest score possible," officials suggested that "responsible" parents should consider the sessions "all-but-mandatory" classes that are "highly encouraged" and "not really optional in reality."

Adam wondered if this meant he'd get a detention for tardiness.

He slipped into 242 and sat in the back.

The voluntary/mandatory teacher was explaining the art of educated guesses. She handed out a reading passage entitled "America Builds a Transcontinental Railroad." Below the passage were several questions with multiple-choice answers.

"This is from a past state test," the teacher said. "Normally you'd read the passage, then pick the right answer for each question. And we will get to that. By next month I'll be standing here with a stopwatch, and you will be reading a passage like this and underlining every key concept in one minute and forty-five seconds. But today I don't want you looking at the reading passage. Today we are going to answer questions without reading the passage. Isn't that fun?"

The students stared blankly at her.

"OK, good," she said. "Now, as we've all heard Mrs. Marris say, our job is to learn to be savvy test takers. Tell me, girls and boys—what rhymes with *savvy*?"

They sat quietly going through the alphabet in their heads.

"Gravy?" said a boy.

"No," said the teacher. *"Gravy. Savvy.* No."

"Navy?" said another boy.

"I was going to say that," said a girl in the front row.

The teacher shook her head.

They looked confused.

"Nothing," said the teacher, "nothing rhymes with *savvy.*"

"No, it doesn't," said a boy. "'Twinkle, twinkle little *nothing* / How I wonder what you're *savvy.*' No way that rhymes."

"My point," said the teacher, "is no word rhymes with *savvy.*"

"I thought no word rhymed with *orange,*" said a girl.

"That's not my point," said the teacher. *"Savvy* rhymes with nothing; it's out there all alone. And that's how you must be when you take the test.

112

Savvy as a fox in the forest at twilight. You're out there all alone against these wise guys from the state who made up this test and would like nothing better than to have you fail. And you, the savvy test takers, must figure out how to outsmart them.

"For multiple-choice questions, there are four answers," she continued. "Two will be way off, one will be close, and one will be right. What does the savvy test taker do?"

"Pick the right answer," said a boy.

"Absolutely not," said the teacher. "That's the smart test taker. We haven't got that far. I'm talking savvy."

The girl in front suggested eliminating the two answers that are way off.

"Now there's a savvy test taker," the teacher said. "Good for you, Miss Savvy."

She had them look at the first question and put an *X* through the two answers that were way off.

The question asked which two cities the transcontinental railroad linked. "The key," said the teacher, "is the meaning of *transcontinental*." They looked ready to fall asleep; heads were flopping on chests and jerking up. *"Transcontinental?"*

"Across the continent," said Adam.

"I was going to say that," said the girl in front.

"Good," said the teacher. "Let me hear one answer you put an *X* through."

"Paris to New York," said a boy.

"Good," said the teacher. "What would it be if it went from Paris to New York?"

"Sopping wet," said the boy.

"True," said the teacher, "but what word? *Trans . . . Transatl . . . Transatlanti . . .* No one? . . . *Transatlantic*, right?"

"I was going to say that," said the girl in front.

The teacher asked for another wrong answer.

"Chicago to Sacramento," said the girl in front.

"Good," said the teacher.

"I disagree," said a boy. "The question asked which two cities it linked. I guess they mean one on the East Coast and one in California, but it could be true the train linked Chicago and Sacramento, too. So I don't see why that can't be an answer."

The teacher reread the question. "Well, you may have a point . . . No, no, no!" she said, regaining her senses. "You're overthinking. You want to think like the guy from the state making up the test. He's trying to be a little tricky, but not way tricky. I mean, he's no genius—he makes up tests for a living."

*   *   *

It was a little past four when Adam got to 306. He pulled an iced-tea carton from his backpack, stuck in a straw, and took a deep drink. He was dry. The voluntary/mandatory had been even worse than he'd feared. In the time they'd practiced educated guesses, Adam could have built the stupid railroad. Over the weekend Adam had tried convincing his father that he didn't need the voluntary/mandatory classes, since he had done so well on the test last year, but boy, did that set his father off. "Young man," his father had said, "today's four-pluser is tomorrow's two. Don't ever forget that. You cannot let your guard down; people are always gunning for the four-pluser." Adam had tried explaining that the test wasn't hard, but his father started shouting, "Hubris! Hubris! Do you know what hubris is, Adam?" Adam didn't, so he blurted out something ridiculous, ran up the stairs, stomping each one extra loud, rushed to his room, and slammed the door. Later his parents took him out for soft ice cream, but he still had to go to voluntary/mandatory.

Jennifer walked in. When she saw Adam was

there first, she looked at her watch in mock astonishment and they both smiled. He was happy to see her.

"What's hubris?" Adam asked.

"Overblown pride," said Jennifer. "Why?"

"Nothing," said Adam. "You think Phoebe's going to show?"

"I think she will," said Phoebe, walking in. "Sorry I'm late, but my voluntary/mandatory got out late." She thudded down her backpack, then flopped on a couch. "Got your note," Phoebe said to Jennifer. "Actually, got it twice. Very weird. A girl came up to me in the hall, said, 'This is from my sister,' and gave me the note. Then at recess the girl came up again, said, 'This is from my sister,' and handed me the same note. I kept wondering how many times she'd come back. I felt like I was in a video someone kept rewinding."

"They're twins," said Jennifer with a laugh. "My sisters. Two different girls, two different notes."

Phoebe nodded and pretended to get it. She knew from dealing with her older brothers that you have to let a lot go by. She understood Jennifer and Adam would never let her in on their inside jokes.

Jennifer stood up. "Got to go," she said.

Adam looked panicked. "You're leaving?" he said. "We have to talk about the smile story."

"You don't need me," said Jennifer. "One coeditor per reporter is plenty. We're studying the Constitution in Social Studies. Two coeditors per reporter is a violation of the Eighth Amendment—cruel and unusual punishment."

Adam glanced at Phoebe. He was determined to be upbeat, so it was hard to think of anything to say.

"Did you like it?" asked Phoebe.

"Like what?" said Adam.

"The Eddie the janitor story," said Phoebe. "Was it OK?"

"Oh yeah," said Adam. "It was good. We didn't tell you? I thought we said something. Nice job."

"Really?" said Phoebe. "You liked it?"

Adam nodded.

"YES!" squeaked Phoebe, jumping out of her chair and twirling around. She had hoped the *Dash* editors would think the Eddie story was so great they'd call her right away at home and admit they'd made a terrible mistake not putting her on the Spotlight Team. But days had passed with no word. "Did you like the part about the birds and the toothbrush and spoon?"

"Yeah," said Adam. "I did."

"And the boy in the wheelchair. Wow. Pretty great, huh? I had to go back five times before Eddie told me that."

"Yeah, it was good," said Adam.

"I have lots more in my notebooks," said Phoebe. "Want another page or two?"

"No," said Adam. "Length is perfect."

"You really liked it?" said Phoebe. "You're not just saying it because you feel sorry for me?"

"No," said Adam. "I adored it. Loved it. Would marry it if I could."

"Could it go front page?" asked Phoebe.

"Don't know yet," said Adam.

"I think it could be a very strong front-page story," said Phoebe.

"We'll see," said Adam.

"I have great ideas for front-page art," she said. "We could get a front-page photo of Eddie with the two mourning doves. Or—"

"I DON'T KNOW!" screamed Adam. "STOP, PLEASE, JUST STOP FOR A MINUTE! LET'S TAKE A

118

TALKING BREAK." Adam sat for a few seconds, composing himself. He had been concentrating so much on getting Jennifer to stop being mad at him, he'd forgotten what Phoebe was like. He had let his guard down. This was a good reminder for any co-editor. Just because someone wrote nicely didn't mean they were a pleasure to be around.

Adam asked how the smile contest went. "I was flipping channels," he said, "and caught News 12. It looked kind of funny, all those kids smiling."

"It was weird," said Phoebe. She pulled out a sheet of paper from her backpack. "So far, I've written the start," she said. "I'm not sure about it. I feel a little—I don't know—sneaky. The story is supposed to be about kids working hard smiling to win five hundred dollars for a good cause. That's what the press release said. And I think the people in charge tried to do good, but this lady Phyllis—there was something so phony about the whole thing."

She handed Adam the lead. The story began:

> The Tremble Dental Association recently held a smile contest at the mall to promote healthy teeth and remind people that October is Dental Health Month. At the

start of the competition—which lasted over four hours before a champion smiler was crowned—Dr. Artimus Cooper, DDS, issued a grave warning. "If we don't control our kids' sweets intake," he said, "we could be looking at a billion new cavities in America in twenty years."

Well, thanks to the dental association smile contest, we are well on our way to those billion new cavities. In fact, at the rate those smilers at the mall were consuming candy and soda, they themselves may get a billion new cavities.

Trying to smile for several hours is exhausting. Where did the smilers get their energy? Candy. Tons of candy. Suzy Mollar, Number 12, winner of the five-hundred-dollar grand prize, ate almost an entire ten-pound bag of M&M's during her four hours and three minutes of smiling and drank soda as well. She declared sugar the key. "My mom poured those M&M's down my throat," she said. "Yipes! My toes were tingling; I could feel my heart pounding. I was riding a sugar wave to victory."

When he finished, Adam said, "Geez, that really happened?"

Phoebe nodded.

"You sure?" asked Adam.

"Want to see the photos?" said Phoebe.

"You have photos already?" said Adam.

Phoebe nodded. "I was so nervous they wouldn't come out, I made my mom go to One-Hour Photo."

He looked through the pile, shaking his head, then held one up. "This girl with the Number 12 tooth and the M&M bag stuffed over her head— Suzy Mollar?"

"Tremble Dental Association smile champion," said Phoebe.

"Boy," said Adam. "Save us from Dental Health Month, huh?"

They were quiet, then Adam said, "You did great, Phoebe. You did it again. I have to admit, this is amazing. It'll be wonderful when it's done."

Phoebe nodded.

Adam braced himself for another Phoebe victory dance, but she just sat there. "Anything wrong?" he asked.

"I don't know," said Phoebe. "This one doesn't feel great. When I did Eddie—it was a hero's story long overdue for telling. But this one's going to upset people."

"Well, it should," said Adam. "These dental people sound like idiots."

"I guess," said Phoebe. "It's just harder to say that if you've met them face-to-face. I mean Dr. Cooper and Phyllis, they weren't trying to be stupid. This Phyllis, she wanted to give me an award."

"Were they the ones standing in front of the smilers on News 12?" said Adam. "They looked awfully ready to take credit for the event."

Phoebe nodded.

"How come News 12 didn't have the candy?" asked Adam.

"They stayed a minute and left," said Phoebe. "They had some big four-hundred-pound story to go to."

"They're a disaster," said Adam.

"I don't know," said Phoebe. "Maybe that's what people want. Happy news."

"No," said Adam. "It's not your job to write what Phyllis wants. If that's what we did, we could have Phyllis do the story and call it 'Phyllis's World.' Our job as reporters is to tell the truth as we see it. It has to be backed by facts, but that's what good newspapers do. That's why people read newspapers. They trust reporters to be honest about what they see. They trust reporters to ask questions that everyone else is too embarrassed to ask or too afraid. Phoebe, you are the public's eyes and ears. You, Phoebe, take your best shot at telling them the truth about what's going on in their town."

Phoebe didn't look like the public's eyes and ears. She looked shrunken. "Maybe we could do the story without their names," Phoebe said weakly. "So Phyllis and her husband wouldn't be embarrassed. Couldn't we just say 'dental officials'?"

"Oh no," said Adam. "No way. We have to use names. That's good journalism. Using real names holds us to a higher standard. It means we have to be telling the truth about people. If we make up the names, how can the reader be sure we're not making up facts, too?"

Phoebe didn't say a word.

"Come on, Front-Page Phoebe," said Adam. "I'm not used to you being so quiet. You OK?"

"I guess," said Phoebe. "I just keep thinking, When Phyllis reads it—I'm dead."

chapter 8

The Willows

By the time Adam set out for 48 Grand Street to see what he could learn about Miss Minnie Bloch and her gift to the school, he knew a lot more about the Willows. As promised, Danny had dropped off the old newspaper with the historical articles. "Look it over," Danny said. "It's good background."

There was one black-and-white photo, in particular, that Adam could not stop staring at. Dated "circa 1900," it was taken in front of the train station and showed a woman with a dress that went from the top of her neck to her ankles, sitting in a horse-drawn wagon with a sign painted on the sideboard that read, TREMBLE RIVER TAXI & LIVERY. In the wagon were four smiling children, three girls in long dresses with big bows in their hair, and a boy, about Adam's age, in a white shirt, tie, pressed shorts, and high stockings. The woman and her children were white. In front of the carriage, beside several large trunks, stood several men and women, staring seriously into the camera, half of them white, the rest black.

The photo caption said, *Early Tremble River Summer Residents with Servants.*

Adam read the articles describing Tremble's progress from a sleepy summer community to a prosperous year-round suburb full of adults taking the train into the city for work. But it was the photo that he kept thinking about on this October afternoon, as he biked up Grand toward Minnie Bloch's house. The woman and children in the taxi, waiting to be driven to their new summer cottage—they lived by the river, where Adam lived. And the servants who carried the trunks—they were the ancestors of people who now lived in the Willows.

He was pretty sure this was what Danny had wanted him to understand.

Adam had never been up these streets, never had

a play date or carpooled with anyone from this neighborhood. As he biked, he noticed a few kids who looked familiar from school or sports, but he didn't know their names.

The houses were just as Danny had described, small and rectangular, going back deeper than they were wide. Adam could see why they were called shotgun houses. Maybe half looked good, with flower boxes and potted plants, but a lot needed a paint job and raking. Riding into the wind, Adam could smell the sewage plant.

Number 48 Grand was boarded up. A sheet of plywood was nailed over each window. Adam was disappointed. He'd been hoping someone would be living there who would know about Miss Bloch. In the small front yard, there was a real estate sign that said SOLD. On the way over, Adam had noticed four or five of those same SOLD signs in front of boarded-up homes. He pulled out a notebook and began writing a description of the house.

"Can I help you?" asked a woman standing on the front steps of the house next door. Adam startled. He hadn't noticed anyone when he rode up.

"Lordy," said the woman, "you're not one of those real estate agents buying up the Willows, are you?" She had a big wad of something in her mouth and spit a glob of dark-colored, menacing-looking liquid from her cheek into a white Styrofoam cup.

"Oh no, ma'am," said Adam. "I'm definitely not a real estate anything."

"Didn't think so," she said. "Didn't think they were starting them that young, although you never know when it comes to those snakes. If I see one more house bought and boarded up on this street, I'm going to get out my bazooka." She spit more dark juice into the cup. "How come you're scribbling all them words in that notebook?" she asked.

When Adam explained he was a reporter, her eyes bulged. "You're not from that Bolandvision News 12 are you?" she yelled. "I hate that news almost as much as I hate that Sumner J. Boland. They never tell the real truth. All news all the time, my ass. That is the sorriest news I ever seen."

"I know what you mean," said Adam. "It's pretty bad." He told her he was from the *Dash* and was trying to write about a Miss Bloch who used to live there.

The woman's expression seemed to soften. "Why on earth would you want to do a story on Minnie?" she asked. "She's dead. Won't be much of a story."

"She left money to our school," said Adam. "I

was just trying to find out more about her. No one seems to know much."

"You go to Harris?" said the woman. "Why didn't you say so, son? I guess I could tell you a thing or two about Minnie. There's things to tell." She held out her hand. "Want some?"

"I don't know," said Adam. "What is it?"

The woman took a fistful of brown fibery material from a pouch, packed it into a neat, small pile, and stuck it in her cheek. "Chewing tobacco," she said.

Adam said he'd better not.

"Oh, you're one of those good little boys," said the woman, winking at him. "That's all right. Some good boys turn out fine, too. Well, go ahead, fire away, Gridley. What you want to know?"

Adam wasn't prepared for her directness. What he wanted to know was how Miss Bloch had lived in a house like 48 Grand yet had all that money to give away. But he was afraid if he asked, this woman would feel insulted, like she lived in a crappy house, too. So he just looked at her, a little stupidly he feared, trying to think of some way to get the conversation going and lead up to the big idea slowly. Where was Jennifer when he needed her? She'd know what to say.

The woman waited, but the boy appeared to have turned mute, so she started rubbing her forehead, making circular motions with her hands. "Ooba, ooba, wha, wha, moe, moe," she chanted, her eyes closed now. "Let me see. It's coming to me." She opened her eyes. "Now I'm not a professionally trained journalist like yourself, son. But I think if I was, what I'd like to know is how someone could live in a dump like the Willows and have all that money to give away."

"Yes!" said Adam. "I mean, no. It's not a dump; it's just . . . I didn't mean for you to think, that I think . . ."

"Calm down, child," said the woman. "It's about time someone asked. I been wondering when somebody would be smart enough to come around. Been waiting a few years now. And who's the wise man comes knocking? Little boy, all skin and bones. What's your name, anyway?"

He told her. "Adam," she repeated. "That fits. The first man. Lot of pressure, going first. The Bible Adam—one wrong bite and he was exhaled from Paradise. Always felt that was a little rough. Just natural the first would make a few mistakes. How are you about making mistakes?"

"We try to fact-check all our stories," said Adam.

"Then we should be fine," said the woman. "Now, Adam, I know you aren't the kind of boy who chews tobacco. Would you be the kind of boy who likes cocoa and marshmallows?" Then Mrs. Betty Willard invited Adam Canfield into her house and walked him straight down the center hallway to her kitchen table.

"Minnie left school at thirteen," began Mrs. Willard, bringing over a mug with a couple dozen of those little bobbing marshmallows at the top that Adam loved. "Must have been fifty years she worked as a jewelry polisher, took every lick of overtime she could get. Wasn't easy for her, neither. She left home before dawn to catch three buses to the factory, and by the time I seen her walking back up the street, it was dark.

"In her ninety-two years, that woman never traveled outside Tremble County," Mrs. Willard continued. As far as Mrs. Willard knew, Miss Bloch took just a single pleasure trip in her life, to East Tremble, to see the mall when it was new. "Afterward, Minnie told me she was offended by all the ways people wasted money. That Minnie was mighty tight with a dollar."

Miss Bloch lived her first forty-five years with her mother, who, according to Mrs. Willard, was a German immigrant and very conceited about having been the head household servant for one of the richest, oldest Tremble families. The mother dominated Minnie's life, Mrs. Willard explained, and after her death, Minnie lived the next twenty-five years with her brother, who also dominated. After his death, she lived alone.

Mrs. Willard stood and looked out the sliding door to her backyard. "Tell me this, Adam," she said. "You embarrassed by any silly little things that scare you?"

He stopped taking notes. "Yeah," he said. He felt funny talking about it, but since a reporter asked so many personal questions, it seemed like he should answer a few. "Sometimes I get scared our house is going to burn down," he said softly. "At night I'll see a car's headlights on the street from my upstairs window and think it's fire."

"Well, that's how Minnie was," said Mrs. Willard. "Except she couldn't control it good as you.

Everything scared her. Bugs, thunder, animals, men."

"Kids, too?" asked Adam. "She must have liked kids. She gave money to our school."

"Not really," said Mrs. Willard. "When my kids was little, she used to holler if they ran into her yard to fetch a ball. But she was a funny bird. You know, she'd plan weeks ahead for Halloween, was the only one I knew in the Willows who gave out full-size candy bars.

"After she retired," Mrs. Willard continued, "her only regular contact with the outside world was yours truly. Every morning she'd call me at nine-thirty: 'Hello, Betty. I made it through another night.' The older that lady got, the cheaper she got. She watched television in the dark to save on electricity, said she could see fine from the streetlight. She dusted with a mop made from old underclothes and a coat hanger, caught water that dripped from the kitchen faucet and used it to wash dishes."

"Geez," said Adam. "Sounds like *Little House on the Prairie.* She doesn't seem like a rich lady."

"That's what I thought," said Mrs. Willard. "You wait here. I need to get something." She disappeared down the hall into a bedroom. Adam looked at her backyard. Mrs. Willard had several bird feeders in a tree, and on one a squirrel was hanging upside down, stealing food.

When Mrs. Willard returned, she had a stack of browned papers tied with a silk ribbon.

"Before I forget," said Adam, "got a photo of her in there? I'd like it for the paper."

"Never let me take her picture," said Mrs. Willard. "Said she was too ugly—her face would break the camera. A few times I asked about family photo albums, but she claimed they was destroyed in a flood."

"Check these out," she said, handing Adam a pile of receipts.

"Are they from her funeral?" Adam asked.

"They are," said Mrs. Willard. "For five years, the first Sunday of every month, she rode two buses to Longwood Memorial to pay off her cemetery plot on the installment plan. When she died, she did not owe a cent to a soul. She'd even had her name and birth date carved on the tombstone. All the cemetery had to do was add the expiration date."

"Did you go to the funeral?" asked Adam.

"The hearse driver, a minister, and me—that's all," said Mrs. Willard. "From the minister's speech,

I could tell he didn't know her. There was no write-up in the paper, neither. And that would've been the end of the story, except about a year later I get a call from a lawyer, says a Miss Minnie Bloch had named me as executor of her will, asked if I'd come to his office downtown to sign papers."

"You saw the will?" asked Adam.

Mrs. Willard nodded. "You know that woman had five savings accounts and never touched any of them? Lived off the four hundred and fifty dollars she got from Social Security each month."

"How much was there?" said Adam.

"Nearly half a million dollars," said Mrs. Willard, and glancing at Adam's face, she added, "Knocked my socks off, too."

He wanted to know how Miss Bloch had picked the charities.

"As best I can tell, most were just places that helped out when she needed them. She left money to the Tremble rescue squad—they took her to the hospital a bunch of times. The volunteer fire department pumped out her basement after a flood. Nurses at the hospital named in Minnie's will were kind when her brother was dying. The animal shelter—"

"That one I know," said Adam. "How about Harris?"

"Well," said Mrs. Willard, "Minnie had very peculiar ideas about the schools. Since she had no kids, I think all she knew was what she saw on the TV news—teenage suicide, drugs, eating disorders, bomb threats, sexual diseases, guns in the classrooms. She used to say to me, 'Betty, it's a miracle those children get out of high school alive.'"

Mrs. Willard believed that Miss Bloch had picked Harris because Mrs. Willard's two children—both now grown and moved away—had gone there years ago.

By now Adam was on his second notepad, scribbling a mile a minute.

"What's that, pharmacy writing?" asked Mrs. Willard. "You take shorthand?"

"Just my own scribble," said Adam.

"You can read that?" asked Mrs. Willard. "I'm getting wore out just watching you. Any more questions? I got errands to run."

This made Adam nervous. He had been holding the most important questions for last and now worried he might miss his chance.

"Just a few," he said, trying to sound casual. He wondered if Mrs. Willard happened to remember how much Miss Bloch left to Harris.

"I believe it was seventy-five thousand dollars," she said.

He wondered if Miss Bloch happened to have included instructions in the will about how the money should be spent.

"My memory is she left it a little general," said Mrs. Willard. "Guess she didn't want to restrict things too much. The will said something about using the money to generally improve the life of deserving children who do not have an easy time of it. To be honest, I think Minnie was thinking of someone like herself when she was a girl."

"The money was supposed to be spent on kids?" Adam asked.

"Oh yes," said Mrs. Willard. "Definitely for kids. That was the whole idea."

Adam needed to see that will. He asked for the lawyer's name.

"I should have his card here," she said, digging through the pile. "Nice old man. Jewish fellar, I think." She found it, and Adam copied down the name and number.

"One more thing," said Mrs. Willard. "Minnie wanted people to know in some little way that the money was from her. Nothing big or showy. But the will says something about giving her recognition — you know, a plaque or a scholarship named for her."

"Or a story in the newspaper?" asked Adam.

Mrs. Willard paused. "I didn't think of that," she said. "But, yes, I guess a story in the paper about Minnie's gift would cover it. That why you're here?"

"Yes and no," said Adam. "Yes and no."

chapter 9
Three Options, All Rotten

Adam couldn't wait to tell Jennifer all the great stuff he'd found out about Minnie Bloch, but he was getting nowhere with the Herbs. It wasn't from lack of trying. They had become a daily item on his To Do list:

Practice baritone
Science project abstract due
Voluntary/mandatory 3 P.M.
Check mashed potato results
Call Herbs

Whenever he called and it was a man, he was sure it was a Herb. But each time, those men, they denied being Herbs. Adam was keeping a tally sheet. Three times he had "just missed them." Four times they were in a meeting. Twice they were on their way in from the field. More than once Adam had asked if there wasn't someone beside a Herb who could help him. "There has to be somebody in a big place like Code Enforcement who could answer one simple question," Adam had said.

"Oh no, honey," the woman had replied. "One thing you learn when you devote your life to code enforcement: nothing is simple. But listen, you keep trying. I recognize your voice. You're one of our regulars. You've been close several times. I have a good feeling about this; I think it's going to happen for you."

And then Adam hit pay dirt. He was up early Monday — his before-school/after-school voluntary/mandatory that day was before school. He hit auto dial. The phone rang once.

"Yeah," a man's voice said.

"Herb Green!" said Adam, trying to sound like a long-lost friend.

"The one and only," said Herb Green.

Adam could not believe his good luck. He'd almost guessed Herb Black.

"Adam Canfield here," said Adam, determined not to miss a beat. "Herb, just had a quick question for you on this new deal on accessory structures in the front half of housing lots—200-52.7A." There was quiet on the other end, but Adam was not about to allow Herb Green any wiggle room. "Wanted to know what sort of structures you'll be applying that to, Herb."

More quiet. "I know you're the man they look to for interpretations of the law," continued Adam. "And I know accessory structures are your specialty. Just wanted to see where we're heading on this one, Herb."

Adam wouldn't let himself exhale; he didn't want to miss a syllable of anything Herb Green said.

And then Herb Green began, speaking slowly and carefully. "It's true, accessory structures are my specialty," he said. "And it's true I do handle *some* code interpretations. But unfortunately, the accessory structure code is not a code interpretation I handle."

Adam could not believe it. This wasn't fair. He had played by the rules, caught a Herb, and now that Herb was trying to squirm free. Adam was losing strength for this. All the juice was going out of him. "Who would that person be?" said Adam quietly.

"Herb Black," said Herb Green.

"Let me guess," said Adam. "Herb Black is in a meeting."

"No, he's not," said Herb Green.

"I just missed him," said Adam.

"No," said Herb Green.

"Out in the field?" said Adam.

"No, he's right here," said Herb Green. "Want to talk to him?"

"Well, yes," said Adam. "That would be nice."

"Hang on," said Herb Green. "I'm going to put you on hold a second and have Herb Black pick up."

Adam felt exhilarated. At last. It just took persistence. All the great reporters had it. These Herbs, they didn't seem like such awful guys after all, probably just overworked. He felt bad for prejudging them.

Adam waited. The phone at Code Enforcement played music while he held. It was a radio station, Q-104, the Dove. His grandmother's favorite. Hard listening for Adam. Something called "Muskrat Love" was on. A minute passed, then two. A new song came on. Something called "We've Only Just

Begun." Even harder listening. Five minutes passed. Suddenly the music stopped. The line went quiet. Adam tensed. This was it.

There was a dial tone. A dial tone! Was this some kind of sick joke? He frantically pressed redial. The phone rang five times. Adam kept thinking, Pick up, pick up. A recording came on. The Code Enforcement office was closed, the recording said, please call back during nine-to-five business hours.

Even from across the lunchroom, Jennifer could see Adam was in a foul mood. He looked like a character in the comics with three little dots over his head and a black cloud where his thought bubble should be. He'd placed his baritone case on the lunch table in front of him, so it looked like he was sitting behind the Great Wall of China. When Jennifer took a seat across from him, he was totally hidden from view.

"Like some company?" she asked, sliding his baritone case just enough to peek at him.

He didn't look up. She pulled out a straw, figured hitting him with a spitball might cheer him up, but then thought better of it. "You OK?" she asked.

No response.

"How's lunch?" she tried.

"I don't know!" Adam barked. "I can't tell what it is."

"Boy, what's wrong?" she said. "You are in a rotten mood."

"It's the Herbs," he said. "They're driving me crazy. I hate them! It's like I'm having an allergic reaction to the Herbs."

"Well, then don't eat that stuff; we can split my lunch," she said. She glanced at his tray. It appeared to be something with noodles, maybe beef goulash supreme. "They overdo the sauce," said Jennifer. "They coat that stuff in herbs just so they can call it goulash *supreme.*"

Adam picked up his plate, and for a moment, Jennifer thought he might crack it over her head, but instead he wagged it at her. "Not these herbs!" he yelled, noodling his finger through the goulash. "The code enforcement Herbs! The accessory structure Herbs! The 200-52.7A Herbs! The basketball hoop Herbs!"

"Shhh," she whispered, trying to calm him down. Kids were staring. "I'm sorry," said Jennifer. "I didn't know you meant Herbs with a capital *H.*"

"Do you have any idea how many times I've

143

called those Herbs with a capital *H*?" said Adam. "I'll tell you exactly." He unzipped his backpack and yanked out a piece of paper. Pistachio nutshells went flying everywhere. He held up his tally sheet documenting each attempt to get hold of the Herbs.

"You're wasting your time," Jennifer said softly.

"Wasting my time?" said Adam. "Listen, babe-o, this was your story. You're the one with the lawyer daddy who knows all about zoning . . ."

Babe-o? thought Jennifer. He was calling her *babe-o*? Normally Jennifer would not take *babe-o* from Adam, but she could see the boy was in pain and she needed to get him back on track. "It's a great story," she said. "But we're not going to get it over the phone. You're just kidding yourself, making all those calls."

Adam slumped in his seat like a goulash noodle.

"They're dodging you," Jennifer continued. "You think the Herbs want to give notice to every kid in Tremble that the hoops are coming down? They'll have a riot on their hands. We just have to go to their office in the county building. They're public officials. We are the public. They have to talk to us. We just have to catch them first. We are going to have to park

144

ourselves in their office until they show up. That's how Woodward and Bernstein did it."

"Who's Woodward Ann Bernstein?" Adam asked glumly.

"Famous investigative reporter team for the *Washington Post*," said Jennifer. "Their Watergate stories forced Richard Nixon to resign as president."

"Great," said Adam. "Only one trouble. I bet they didn't have before-school/after-school voluntary/ mandatory. I bet they're not in jazz band or Odyssey of the Mind or Geography Challenge or —"

"I know when we can do it," said Jennifer.

Adam unfolded a thick pack of stapled papers. "Have you looked at this list Mr. Landmass gave us to memorize for the geography tournament?" he asked. "I'm still in the *E*'s. I don't know where Eritrea is."

"Northern Africa," said Jennifer.

"I don't know where Ernakulam is," said Adam.

"Southern India," said Jennifer.

"I didn't even know the Erzgebirge were mountains," said Adam.

"On the German-Czech border," said Jennifer. "Relax. We'll study together. We can do it on the bus to the county building."

"When?" asked Adam.

Jennifer reminded him there was a half day of school later that week for teacher training workshops. Adam looked away. He'd been hoping to spend the day putting together a bunch of kids for a huge game of manhunt on his street. A rare unprogrammed day of fun. "I've never ridden the bus," Adam mumbled.

Jennifer had. Several times. "My live-in babysitter used to take me," she said. "We'd go to the mall. The N-7. You pick it up at Phil & Sol's Citgo. You transfer to the N-24. Goes right by the county buildings on the way to the mall. It's slow but kind of neat. I loved it when I was little. It's like a secret world. You know who rides the bus? People you don't normally notice. Nannies, cleaning ladies, the dry-cleaner workers—"

"Jewelry polishers," Adam said.

"Sure," said Jennifer. "And it's like, they act different when they're together, like a mask comes off and you see the people they actually are. Kind of like Phoebe's story on Eddie the janitor."

"Kind of like Miss Minnie Bloch," said Adam.

Jennifer gave him a funny look. "No," she said. "Rich people don't ride the bus."

"Minnie Bloch did," Adam said.

And he began to tell Jennifer about Miss Bloch and her gift to Harris.

There was so much to tell, he fed it to her in installments, finishing after school, in 306. For a long while, Jennifer was quiet. "Boy, you were right," she finally said. "There was a lot more to it. What do you think Marris did with the seventy-five thousand dollars?"

Adam shook his head. "Don't know," he said. He'd been wondering about that a lot. The Willows lady was so sure the money was supposed to be for kids, but Adam could not think of any new kid project at Harris. Maybe Marris had quietly created a scholarship for deserving students, but if so, why hadn't she said something during their interview in the Bunker? Wouldn't she want kids to know so they could apply? A scholarship would be just the thing Marris would make a big deal about.

There was nothing like that. Marris was careful about saying the gift was for "general improvements." That could be anything.

"I smell a rat," said Jennifer.

Adam nodded. But what should they do? The

deadline for the *Dash* October issue was a week away. They still hadn't nailed down the basketball hoop story. Half the articles weren't even typed into the computer. No way they were going to get to the bottom of the Miss Bloch investigation in a week.

Adam and Jennifer figured they had three options.

They could print the Miss Bloch story just the way Mrs. Marris had told it to them in the Bunker interview. Then they could do a second story in the next issue when they had figured out how Marris had really used the money. The problem with that option: they'd be publishing a lie. How could they write that Minnie Bloch was a rich lady who had a happy life and donated her money for "general improvements"?

Or a second possibility was printing a story that included everything the Willows lady told Adam. But that would tip off Marris about their investigation when it was only half done. Marris would have time to destroy any incriminating evidence — and Adam and Jennifer, too.

The third possibility was holding the story. Say nothing about Adam's visit to the Willows. Do more reporting and hopefully figure it all out for the November issue. But that could be a disaster, too.

Marris wanted her version of the story in the paper now. Apparently, she needed to publicize the gift to satisfy Miss Bloch's will. Marris must have decided a story in the *Dash* would be the easiest—and least noticed—way to give Minnie Bloch credit. If Adam and Jennifer told Marris the story wasn't finished, she could go ballistic.

"What a mess," said Adam. "We are definitely not getting out of this alive." Worse yet, the Miss Bloch story was supposed to go on the front page. How would they fill the space?

"I've got something," Jennifer said. "You're going to love this. You know the big, old beautiful houses out on Breckenridge?"

Adam did. They had once been farmhouses, and while the farms were long gone, the rolling green hills and white picket fences were a reminder that Tremble used to be country.

"You know that wooden cow in the front yard of the house where the road bends?" said Jennifer. Adam smiled. Boy, did he. It was a life-size black-and-white plywood cow, and while it wasn't the kind of thing you talked about much, that wooden cow was one of those special things about Tremble.

149

When Adam was little, his father made up a story about the cow. Adam couldn't remember the details—something about a wizard turning a real cow into wood to punish a greedy farmer. But every time they drove by in those days, little Adam would yell, "Daddy, tell the cow story, tell it, Daddy."

"It's stolen," said Jennifer. "Someone stole the wooden cow."

"No," said Adam. "Really? Great story."

"It gets better," said Jennifer. "The owner knows my mom." Jennifer's mother and the woman belonged to the same garden club. The woman mentioned the missing cow at their last meeting, and afterward Jennifer called for more details. The woman was delighted to talk, figured a story might help get the cow back.

"It gets better," said Jennifer. "She's offering a hundred-dollar reward for the return of her cow. No questions asked."

"No questions asked?" said Adam. "I love it. It's like the war on terrorism. Wanted dead or alive, no questions asked! I can't wait to write the headline."

"Whoa," said Jennifer. "My story, my headline."

chapter 10

The End of the World

At the start of Wednesday's class, Mr. Brooks said, "Boys and girls, I have a curriculum-related announcement." He paused. "There will be no World Domination game this year."

They were absolutely shocked, too stunned to say a word at first. Then all the hands shot up at once. What had they done? There had to be some mistake. They'd try harder, they promised. They'd memorize the *Aeneid* in Latin. This just wasn't possible.

"*Excelsior*'s our motto, too," said a girl, "from the Latin, Mr. Brooks, to excel."

"Please," Mr. Brooks said. "It's not your fault. You're as fine a class as any I've had in my forty years of teaching. Or at least you have the potential to reach the summit—from the Latin, as you probably guessed, *summum.*" He coughed, seemed to be stalling. They were hanging on every word, knew that he wouldn't lie to them, not Mr. Brooks.

But what finally came out sounded so lame, Adam felt it might as well be a lie. Mr. Brooks said if he was going to cover all the subject matter for the state history test this year, there wasn't time to play World Domination. In the month that they would have taken to play the game, Mr. Brooks said he could teach them a couple of centuries worth of world history facts that would likely turn up on the state test.

Their hands shot up again, but Mr. Brooks shook his head. "Sorry, it's not up for debate," he said. "This is school policy. We have lots to do. Today we're journeying back to Plato's Academy."

"Please, Mr. Brooks," Adam called out. "Could we just see the game board? Franky Cutty says it's bigger than the tallest guy in the NBA. It isn't really, is it?"

* * *

Like the rest of his class, Adam was heartbroken.
But unlike the others, he felt he had the power to do
something. After school that same day, he went
straight to Mr. Brooks's room. His knock seemed to
startle the teacher, who was stacking the day's
homework into his worn leather briefcase.

Adam explained he was ready to do a story for
the *Dash* about the end of World Domination. "You
don't know how much kids love that game," Adam
said. "How we've been looking forward to it. Even
Franky Cutty—he was like the most with-it kid in
the history of Harris Middle—Franky says it is the
most he ever learned in a class."

Mr. Brooks said nothing.

"We'd all stand behind you, Mr. Brooks," Adam
said. "We'll start petitions; we'll picket. This is
worse than that Justinian I guy you told us about
this morning, shutting down Plato's Academy. We'll
get the policy changed. Does Mrs. Marris know?
We'll get her to help."

Mr. Brooks turned away. When he finally spoke,
his response surprised Adam. In class he was the

153

most powerful, most intimidating, most inspiring teacher Adam had ever known, constantly urging them to be bold in their thinking. Now he looked tired, old, almost fragile. "My dear, dear Adam," he said. "I can't stop you from writing a newspaper article. A person doesn't have to be much of a history buff to know that one of the things that makes our democracy so strong is freedom of the press. But man to man, I'm going to ask you—please don't write a word of what I'm about to say. I'm in no position to talk openly. Do I have your word?"

For a moment Adam thought about doing the story without Mr. Brooks. Adam knew the facts. He could interview kids about their reaction. And then he could put in that Mr. Brooks had refused to comment. Reporters did it all the time. It was just—Mr. Brooks was such a decent man; Adam hated writing a story that would upset him.

So he nodded, and the moment he did, he had a sick feeling.

"For three years," Mr. Brooks said, "I've fought this battle behind the scenes with Mrs. Marris. Yes, that's right, Marris. I tried convincing her that in middle school, instead of racing through three thousand years of history facts, there ought to be the freedom to study fewer historical periods closer up. If a class falls in love with Columbus or Magellan, what's wrong with spending an extra week taking the students onto the decks of those ships through the explorers' journals?

"Marris knows how much students learn from World Domination. There was a time, years ago, she thought it was so great, she got the local paper to do a story. But principals, they go whichever way the wind blows. And right now, we've got a level-five hurricane blowing for state testing.

"I held her off awhile," he continued. "And then the results from last year's test came in. My classes did fine, well above average, but not as high as some of the Tri-River districts where teachers follow the state study guide line by line.

"Marris went berserk. The first week of school, she yanked me out of class, summoned me to the Bunker. She kept screaming that state test results 'damn well do matter,' to taxpayers, politicians, the school board, the media—well, really, to all five billion people on the planet. She said unless I stuck to the state study guide, she would do her best to haul me before the school board and get me fired."

The more Adam listened, the more embarrassed

he felt, like this was stuff a kid shouldn't hear. He looked out the window. The afternoon light already had a tinge of orange; the days were getting shorter, all right. He hated that about the fall. He hated how bad all this was making him feel.

"Adam," Mr. Brooks said softly. "I don't want to be the center of attention in some big political battle. I don't want the school board debating whether my students' scores on the state test mean I'm a good teacher or not. These battles get ugly, personal. The last thing I want is to be pulled through the mud by the likes of Ruth Ellen Marris. She will do anything to win. This may be hard for you to understand, Adam, but I'm a lifelong bachelor and I've been fastidious about keeping my life away from the classroom private. Maybe if I was twenty years younger, if I came of age when society was more . . . more . . . broad-minded, I'd feel I could be a more public person. It's just, I'm near retirement and holding on to my dignity is very dear to me."

Mr. Brooks took a white folded handkerchief from his inside suit coat pocket, dabbed his forehead and around his neck. When he spoke again, his voice was closer to normal. "Don't you worry," he said. "More than anything, it is my job to fuel your curiosity, and we will never stop working at that. Even without World Domination, I will continue to strive to be like those bold Greeks inside the Trojan Horse—full of surprises! All right?"

Adam nodded. He couldn't wait to get away from this man.

"Adam?" said Mr. Brooks. *"Ave atque vale."*

"Yeah, right," mumbled Adam, hurrying out of the room.

The meeting with Mr. Brooks had made Adam late for his after-school voluntary/mandatory. He still didn't know if he could get a detention for being tardy for a class that was "not really optional in reality." He should have asked Mr. Brooks for a pass, but he didn't have the heart to bring it up. Voluntary/mandatory was the last class he wanted to mention to Mr. Brooks.

Adam entered 242 with his head down and walked straight to the back. He kept waiting to hear his name, but when he dared look up, he saw the teacher was distracted. There was a huge smile plastered on her face and her speech sounded giddy. He could barely see her; she was hidden behind towering stacks of workbooks.

"You are witnessing history," the teacher was saying. "You have no idea how lucky you are." She held up one of the workbooks like she was Moses on the Mount and had just been handed the two stone tablets. "This is the first study guide ever published for our state competency test! Until now there have been study guides for the SAT, the SAT IIs, the ACTs, the ACT Comps, the GEDs, the APs, the MCATs, the QRXs, and the LMNOPs. But the state competency test was too new.

"Now we have it," she said, her voice a war cry. "Hot off the presses. The first edition ever. Now we can really get down to business!

"You are the first!" she said hoisting the study guide high over her head again. Adam was impressed with how easily she lifted the book and whirled it around. The thing must have weighed a good five or six pounds. This woman definitely works out, Adam thought.

"We think if you master this guide, it will shoot you twos up to threes and you threes up to fours. We think with this by our side, we can push every last child in Tremble up and over the state competency mountain. We are confident there will not be a single incompetent child left in Tremble!

"This guide would normally cost fifteen dollars and ninety-five cents, plus tax, plus four dollars for shipping, if you ordered online. But it is so important to your futures, to our futures, to all the basic quality-of-life issues in Tremble, that we here at school are providing this book free of charge, thanks to a generous grant from the Boland Foundation."

She had a boy and girl pass out the books. "Write your name on the inside cover," she said. "Make this book your best friend. Know it like you know your family.

"For homework, I want you to read the first chapter, 'The ABCs of Understanding Your State Competency Test.'"

Cooking with Herbs

Thursday was early dismissal for Harris teacher workshops. Adam met Jennifer at the bus stop by Phil & Sol's Citgo at 11:45. They joked they were off to see the Herbs, the wonderful Herbs of Oz. Adam was actually looking forward to riding the bus for the first time, but his buddies were upset when they heard he wasn't going to organize a manhunt game. Living along the river, Adam had the best street for any kind of hiding game. Half the houses were vacation homes for people in the city, and this time of year, no one lived in them during the weekdays or even most weekends. You could run through their backyards, dive into their bushes, shinny up their trees, jump off their garage roofs, climb their fences, and no one yelled at you. Sometimes twenty kids, from fourth grade to eighth, would play four hours straight. For Adam's birthday, they had a manhunt game that lasted until ten at night. He loved the chase. Adam was one of the fastest and hardest to capture, great at deeking out kids. Often he appeared out of nowhere and freed his teammates from jail.

The bus pulled up. Adam bounded up the stairs and handed the driver a dollar bill plus a quarter.

"Can't take that," said the driver.

"It's a dollar twenty-five," said Adam.

The driver shot him a cold stare. "You need exact coins, a token, or a fare card," the driver said, looking away in disgust.

Adam hated not knowing the rules. He felt like an idiot. He looked back to Jennifer, but she didn't have change either. He didn't know what to do.

"Let those kids on," said a woman sitting in a bench seat by the driver. "We're already ten minutes late. Come here, son," she said to Adam. "Guess you're not a regular on the N-7, huh? Hold on." She went into her purse and ripped open a roll

161

of quarters, trading Adam and Jennifer four quarters each for their dollar bills.

Adam thanked her and looked around. Jennifer was right. He was the only white person on the bus.

"You can sit here," said the woman who'd helped them. "No one's going to bite you."

The woman looked at her watch and shook her head. "Going to be late for my next cleaning job," she said. "You know what that lady will think when I walk in fifteen minutes late? *Those people, they don't have the same sense of time in their culture.* She won't actually say it—a good cleaning lady's hard to find, and she don't want to lose me. But I can tell you what that lady won't think. She won't think the N-7's running fifteen minutes late again. That's because her kind's never sat their behinds down on a bus, so how would they know?" She glanced at Adam. "I expect *you* to go back and tell them," she said.

Adam shot her a sideways look like she was crazy.

"Just kidding, baby," she said. "You rich?"

Adam was caught so off-guard, all he could do was mumble.

"Don't be embarrassed," she said. "I wish I was rich. There's nothing I'd like better than to say farewell to the Tremble County Bus Authority. You have a cleaning lady at your house?"

Adam nodded.

"So I guess you're at least a little rich," she said. "Maybe you can answer this. How come these rich ladies I work for, every time I see them, they're in sweatsuits rushing out to their fancy gyms? They want to work out, how come they don't clean the house once in a while? I'm not saying put me out of a job, but I sure wouldn't mind if they washed a floor or vacuumed a rug between my visits. You know what I mean?"

Adam nodded.

"What's your name?" she asked Adam, and hearing the answer, she said, "That Eve sitting beside you?"

"Jennifer," said Jennifer.

"You boyfriend and girlfriend?" asked the woman.

Adam blushed.

"School buddies," said Jennifer.

"That's nice," said the woman. "Friends. Would have been nice if Adam and Eve was like you two, one white, one brown. We'd all be beige by now. Less chance to hate."

163

"I don't know," said Jennifer. "My dad says people always find ways to hate."

The woman nodded. "True," she said. "Still, you know what? I seen the two of you together as we pulled up to the Citgo, I thought, maybe the world is getting a little better. It just takes so-o-o long. I never had a white friend. What you kids up to?"

Jennifer told her they were going to the county building for a school project. "The N-7 to the N-24?" asked Jennifer.

"Oh no," said the woman. "That N-24's gone. They got rid of it last year during budget cuts. People in Tremble, they think their taxes might go up a penny, first thing they do is cut another bus route. You got to take the N-7 to the terminal. Then the Q-13 to the Shell station on Dutch Broadway, where you get the P-104. You make sure you get transfers from the driver." They looked confused. "I should write that down?" she said. Adam handed her his pad and a pen. He was struck by how slowly and carefully she made her letters. "Don't you worry," she said. "You're not sure, you ask. You'd be surprised, most people welcome the chance to perform a small kindness."

She rose to leave. "You have a good day," she said to them. "It was nice meeting such lovely friends."

*　　*　　*

The ride took longer than they expected, over two hours. There was plenty of time to do the geography list. They got all the way to *T*: Tel Aviv, Telescope Peak, Tora Bora.

In the lobby of the county building, a sleepy-looking woman sat at the information desk. Behind her, on the wall, hung a large building directory sign. It listed every department's room number. The sign was crooked, with lots of letters and numbers missing. Instead of *Code Enforcement,* it said "*od Enforcement.*"

"Take the elevator down two floors to LL1," said the woman. "Turn right and walk to the end."

They were surprised the elevator was operated by a human, a man dressed in a blazer; they'd never ridden an elevator where they couldn't press the buttons themselves. The operator pulled a folding metal gate across the opening, then rotated a handle on a wheel to shut the door. Adam was fascinated. He felt like he was in jail. The elevator made whooshing noises and moved slowly. At LL1 the man cranked the handle again, the door opened, and he pulled back the metal gate.

"Od Enforcement, last room on the right," he announced.

Adam and Jennifer looked at him funny, but his expression didn't change.

They were in the subbasement. The hallway had the eerie look of a place with no windows, walls that were white, and lighting that was too bright. The overhead fluorescent fixtures gave off a humming noise.

The door at the end was open. When they stuck in their heads, they were surprised at how small the room was. The furniture was a dirty khaki-green metal. Along the back wall were filing cabinets, the drawers so stuffed, papers and folders stuck out everywhere.

Taking up almost an entire wall was a map of Tremble County. Hundreds of red thumb tacks dotted the map. At the top was written, A.S. PHASE I. There was a red bar graph that went from 0 to 100 percent. The red color was nearly to the top now and someone had scribbled, *Phase I: 98 percent complete!*

No one was sitting at two of the desks, and both were filthy, covered with files, newspapers, pink memo slips, dirty coffee cups, candy wrappers, soda cans, empty pizza boxes, and the remains of several bagels and glazed doughnuts, all forming a coating so thick, Adam couldn't see the desk surface. Each desk had a black rotary dial phone that made Adam's eyes bug out; only once in his life had he seen a phone with a twirl dial—at his grandmother's summer cottage. Both desks had an electric typewriter and an in-basket; there were no computers.

The third desk, the one nearest the door, was so close to the other two that the woman sitting there could put notes into the in-baskets without standing. Not that she couldn't have used the exercise. She was a very, very large woman. And immaculately neat. Her desk shined, it had been dusted so often. The only things on it were a huge bound ledger; a stack of pink message pads; and a copy of *People* magazine's special double issue, the fifty most beautiful people in the world.

The woman was taking a call and hadn't noticed Adam and Jennifer. Adam, however, recognized her voice immediately.

"Honey, I'm sorry, the Herbs are very busy today," the woman was saying to the caller. "I know you're frustrated . . . we all are. . . . Now, don't get upset. That's not going to help. . . . You hold on just a second, I actually think I hear them coming. You may be in luck—this may be the Herbs. . . . I'm

167

going to run over and see if it's them on the far side of the office. . . ."

Adam and Jennifer glanced around, surprised. They hadn't heard a thing, except the fluorescent lights humming. The woman put down the phone but did not budge. She opened her *People* magazine and read the bio of the twenty-seventh most beautiful person in the world. When she'd finished, she picked up the phone. "Still there? . . . Let me catch my breath. . . . I been racing all over, honey. Thought I had one, but it wasn't a Herb. . . . Yes, I could take a message, but I have to warn you . . ."

Adam whispered to Jennifer, "The Herbs, they're terrible about returning phone calls, honey."

"They're terrible about returning phone calls, honey," the woman said into the phone.

Adam whispered to Jennifer: "Code enforcement is thankless work."

The woman said, "Code enforcement is thankless work, honey."

Adam and Jennifer ducked back into the hallway. They listened for the woman to finish, then walked in. She was recording the last call in the ledger on her desk.

She glanced up and started. "God, you scared

me," she said. "I didn't know anyone was here. We don't usually get visitors." She sized them up, then said to Jennifer, "You selling Girl Scout cookies, honey? We do get people your size once in a while, ambitious little girls, mommies work in the building, selling those delicious cookies."

They shook their heads. "We're here to see the Herbs," said Jennifer.

"Which one?" said the woman.

"They're pretty much interchangeable," said Adam.

"Ahhh," said the woman, eyeballing Adam real good. "That they are. . . . Well, as you can see, they're not here right now. Fact is I'm not expecting them back today. They're out doing code enforcement."

"Thankless work, code enforcement," said Adam. "Probably's made them very bitter Herbs."

The woman nodded nervously. She slipped the *People* magazine special issue back into her middle drawer.

"Still having trouble with their stomachs?" asked Adam.

Jennifer leaned over and picked up the remains of a glazed doughnut from a Herb's desk. She'd never felt such a rock-hard doughnut. It must have been there for months. "This could destroy any-body's stomach," said Jennifer, wagging the dough-nut at the woman. "Ever see how much oil's used to cook a doughnut?"

"Look," said the woman. "Maybe you should come back tomorrow. The Herbs might be in then."

"It's OK," said Jennifer. "It took us two hours to get here by bus."

"We'll wait," said Adam.

"As I explained," said the woman, "I don't expect them and—"

"We brought stuff to do," said Adam. He pulled out the geography packet. "Homework," he said. "You wouldn't happen to know where Ufa is located?"

The woman shook her head. She kept glancing at the wall clock. It was nearly three, the universal hour for the afternoon coffee break in government offices. "Sure I can't help you?" said the woman.

"Definitely not," said Adam. "We have a ques-tion about accessory structures in the front half of housing lots. Only the Herbs can do interpretations."

"No one can speak for the Herbs," said Jennifer.

The woman nodded. "Well, generally that's true," said the woman. "But in certain cases I—as

170

third ranking here—am permitted to give a non-binding advisory opinion."

"I don't know," said Adam. "When it comes to code enforcement, nothing is simple."

"That is one way to look at it," said the woman. "The other way we can look at it is 'What the hell, let's give it a shot.'"

Adam glanced at Jennifer, who nodded.

Adam said, "We want to know if the crackdown on accessory structures means no basketball hoops in driveways and on sidewalks."

The woman's face lost its color. "Basketball hoops?" she gasped. "What in the world would make you think that law would apply to basketball hoops? That is a good one."

Adam didn't know whether to laugh or cry. He wanted the hoops saved. But he hated to lose a great story.

"So you're saying basketball hoops are not affected," said Jennifer. "The hoops can stay?"

"Oh no," said the woman. "I didn't say that. You were right, this is way too technical for me. I would not touch basketball hoops with a ten-foot pole. You'll have to ask the Herbs how many basketball hoops will be coming down."

"'How *many* hoops will be coming down,'" Adam repeated. "How *many*."

"Not for her to say," said Jennifer.

The woman was tapping her fingers on the desk. She was really getting fidgety. She opened a drawer, grabbed her pocketbook, and pulled out a pack of Marlboros. "Mind if I smoke? I usually go out for break, but I'm not supposed to if anybody's here."

"Smoke in a government building?" said Jennifer. "Isn't that against the law?"

"What about the effect of secondhand smoke on children?" said Adam. "I don't think that's good."

"I'm sure," said Jennifer, "that would be a violation of the fire code, public health code, and as I think of it, probably your very own building code."

The woman leaped from behind her desk. She was pretty agile for a large woman. She hurried to a closet, yanked out two folding chairs, and placed them beside her desk. "Promise you'll stay in those seats until I get back?" she said. "I won't be long. We only get fifteen minutes. Can I trust you?"

They nodded. "We'll stay in the seats," said Jennifer.

"Terrible things happen to children who lie," said the woman. "Crossies don't count."

172

"No crossies," Adam agreed.

When the woman left, Jennifer put her finger to her lips. She waited for the second hand on the clock to mark a minute. Then, holding the chair against her bottom, she half stood and crab-walked to the door, keeping the chair under her. Ever so slowly she peeked her head into the long corridor. Empty.

"What are you doing?" whispered Adam. "You're walking like that chair's glued on."

"Staying in my seat as promised," said Jennifer. "I once saw this investigative reporters' convention on C-SPAN. The speaker said reporters can't lie, but they don't have to volunteer the whole truth. We told that lady we'd stay in our seats; we didn't say how much the seats might move around. Get busy!"

Adam rolled his eyes but followed her lead. Holding the chair to his butt, he waddled to the wall map. "A.S. Phase I — must be accessory structures," Adam said.

"Albert Einstein reborn," said Jennifer. "Tell me something I don't know."

Adam scanned the map for the words "basketball" or "hoops" but couldn't find anything. It was obvious each red pin stood for an accessory structure. But were they hoops?

Standing half-crouched with the chair tight against his butt, he had trouble seeing the top of the map. But he found the Tremble River, then followed its winding path down to his part of town, locating his street. There were two red pins. That was it! Two red pins! There were two hoops on his street, his and the Corcorans'. He looked at the street next to his, where he knew there were no hoops. No pins! He looked at Jennifer's street. "You the only hoop on your street?" he asked.

"Just us," she said.

"One pin!" said Adam. He tried every friend with a hoop—Kaiser, Weiss, O'Shea, Gross, Ramirez, Capone, Glazer, Carey. A perfect match: one hoop, one pin.

"Got it!" said Adam excitedly.

"Count them," said Jennifer. "Quick."

Adam let out a moan. There were so many pins.

Jennifer said, "Use your estimation skills, boys and girls," and Adam understood. In second grade they'd learned several estimation tricks. If he counted every pin in one part of the map—say one-fifth of it—he could then multiply that total times five and get an estimate for the entire map.

He got busy but before long was distracted by a

174

low whistling from Jennifer. Other people's whistling was so annoying, especially when he didn't know the tune. He tried to put it out of his head but finally whipped around to make a nasty comment and realized Jennifer was frantically waddling her chair back to its original spot. Why did he always turn stupid in emergencies? He pulled his chair tight, then race-waddled back.

They sat still, concentrating on slowing down their breathing. Adam could hear voices in the hall. Men's voices. The Herbs! He could make out bits of conversation. They sounded happy. Adam heard a whoop. They were getting closer. Then one chanted, "Done, done, done."

"All one thousand and forty-eight," said the other.

"Done, done, done."

They burst into the room and Adam was amazed. The Herbs looked exactly like he'd expected, two older men in plaid shirts with potbellies, green work pants, and keys jangling at the hip. The black Herb, Herb Green, was carrying a box of Tasty Choice doughnuts, and the white Herb, Herb Black, had three coffees in a cardboard tray. They practically danced to their desks, giving their visitors big smiles.

"Must be Girl Scout cookie season," said Herb Green, smiling at Jennifer. "We've got a visitor."

"If we'd known," said Herb Black, "we wouldn't have bothered with doughnuts."

"Any new cookie selections this year?" asked Herb Green.

Jennifer hoped her smile didn't look as nervous as it felt. "We're not from the Girl Scouts," she said.

"Actually we're reporters," said Adam.

"Student reporters," said Jennifer, explaining about the *Dash*.

The Herbs asked how they could help.

"We're working on a story on accessory structures," said Adam.

"Oh, we don't need a story on that," said Herb Green, cheerfully. "We already had one in the *Citizen-Gazette-Herald-Advertiser*. Nice little write-up."

Adam nodded. "But it was kind of general," Adam said. "We wanted to know what it meant by accessory structures."

"Mrs. Boland thought it was best to keep things general," said Herb Black.

"Mrs. Boland?" asked Jennifer.

"Mrs. Sumner J. Boland?" asked Adam.

"Herb, is there another Mrs. Boland?" said Herb Green.

"Not that I know of, Herb," said Herb Black. "Mrs. Sumner J. Boland. Chairwoman of the county zoning board. Number-one zoning official in Tremble County. Our boss. The woman we report to. At our last zoning board meeting, she told the reporter from the *Citizen-Gazette-Herald-Advertiser* that it was best to keep the story nice and general. No point of upsetting people. No sense of crowding up a story with a lot of details."

"Herb's right," said Herb Green. "It works out nice. The *Citizen-Gazette-Herald-Advertiser* reporter is very respectful about listening to Mrs. Boland since her husband owns the newspaper. Same with the folks over at Bolandvision News 12. Good reporters. They write what you tell them. Cuts down on confusion. Fewer mistakes. Everything's nice and coordinated."

Adam and Jennifer nodded.

Herb Black put the coffee that said "3 creams/3 sugars" on the woman's desk. Herb Green took his black; Herb Black took his light. "Doughnut?" Herb Green asked the youngsters. "Got plenty. We only needed six, but for a dollar and nine cents extra, you get a dozen. The more you spend, the more you save, ha-ha."

Adam was starving but caught Jennifer's eye and said no thank you. Jennifer felt it wasn't proper to accept any gift—no matter how small—from someone they were writing about: it looked too much like a bribe.

Remembering how hungry he was made Adam agitated. He needed to get this over with and get out of there. It was too much pressure, all this dancing around the subject.

"Listen," he said. "That nice woman who was sitting here—before she left for her break, she told us she didn't know how many basketball hoops would be coming down because of the new enforcement policy."

Herb Green was about to bite into a cream-filled when he abruptly stopped and put his doughnut down. "She told you that?" said Herb Green.

Adam nodded. "She said we'd have to ask the Herbs how many hoops would be coming down."

"She said that?" asked Herb Black.

The two reporters nodded.

The Herbs looked at each other. "You want me to handle this, Herb?" said Herb Black.

"All yours, Herb," said Herb Green.

"I want to be clear," said Herb Black. "This crackdown does not affect hoops in backyards or playground hoops. It does not affect indoor hoops. It's only outdoor freestanding hoops in the front part of a housing lot."

"Just driveway hoops on poles and sidewalk hoops?" said Jennifer.

"Exactly," said Herb Black. "That's all."

"You know how many that would be?" asked Adam.

"Not many," said Herb Black.

"Maybe a thousand?" asked Adam.

The Herbs glanced at each other.

"About," said Herb Green.

"About one thousand and forty-eight?" said Jennifer.

The Herbs didn't look quite so jolly anymore. "That is the final tally," said Herb Black. "That is the number we just came up with today. You going to write all that in your little newspaper?"

Adam and Jennifer nodded.

"Whew," said Herb Black. "I don't know."

"You might want to check with Mrs. Boland," said Herb Green. "She likes to be in charge of what goes in the news."

"You understand," said Herb Black.

"We understand," said Jennifer.

"We definitely understand," said Adam.

They thanked the Herbs. It took all of Adam's and Jennifer's willpower not to cartwheel down the hall. As they neared the elevator, Adam whispered, "We did it."

"Shhh," said Jennifer. "Let's get out of here."

They pressed the "up" button. Finally, the arrow lit up, the door opened, and there, behind the metal gate, stood the very large woman from od Enforcement.

A chill went through Adam and Jennifer. She stood in their way.

Then she smiled and stepped aside. "Got tired of waiting for those Herbs, I bet. Knew you would. Got to go a mighty long ways to catch a Herb."

"You aren't kidding," said Jennifer. "The N-7 . . ."

"To the Q-13 . . ." said Adam.

"To the P-104," said Jennifer. As the metal gate closed, they waved and Adam said, "*Ave atque vale,* honey."

chapter 12

The October Issue

Adam and Jennifer knew it would be a long, hard weekend finishing the October issue. They'd heard horror stories from past editors about getting the paper out and planned to spend every free moment at Adam's house. He had the best computer, complete with a scanner for photos.

The *Dash* had three students who typed stories on their home computers, then e-mailed them to Adam. Even if they wanted to, the typists could not have worked in 306. Newsroom computers were not hooked into the Internet. Mrs. Marris had forbidden it. When Jennifer had asked about getting the room wired, Mrs. Marris gave her a big speech about how overrated the Internet was and how most kids wasted their time playing violent games or surfing adult websites. "How long do you think I'd be principal," Mrs. Marris said to Jennifer, "if I came in some morning and one of your clever little reporters had plastered Harris with printouts of naked web babes?"

To assist them in laying out the pages, Adam's parents had bought him Pagination Made EZ software. At the top of the first page, he programmed in the banner typeface, THE DASH. On the same line, in a box at the right top, he typed, *October Edition.* On the next line, he typed, *Harris Elementary-Middle School.*

Then came the real work. Adam and Jennifer spent Friday night arguing about what the front page should be. Both agreed the basketball story had the hottest news, and they placed it at the top right side of page 1, with a large headline: "Your Hoop's Coming Down!" The story carried a double byline, by both Adam and Jennifer, and was continued inside, taking up nearly two pages.

They disagreed about what story should go on the top left of page 1; Adam wanted the missing plywood cow and the hundred-dollar reward; Jennifer favored Eddie the janitor.

While Jennifer agreed that a hundred-dollar reward would create more buzz than Eddie, she felt there were other considerations. "We don't want two stories at the top that aren't about Harris," she said. "We need balance."

So they put Eddie on top and the hundred-dollar reward right below it. Jennifer wanted Phoebe's smile contest to run under the basketball piece, but Adam said he had something else.

That afternoon on the bus ride home, he had dashed off a story about the new state test study guides. It was only fifty-seven words long and described how the guidebooks were being made available free of charge thanks to a generous grant from the Boland Foundation. Adam's headline read simply, "Free Help!"

Jennifer was surprised. "You hate that testing stuff," she said. "Now you're Mr. Test Prep?"

"Trust me," said Adam. "We're going to need it when Marris realizes there's no story on Miss Bloch's gift to the school."

Along the bottom they stripped the smile story, with the headline "Dental Contest Sugarcoated."

They picked three photos for page 1. Two were by Front-Page Phoebe: Eddie with the two saved mourning doves and smile champion Suzy Mollar with the M&M bag stuffed over her head.

They also ran the cow's photo, an old snapshot the owner had passed along to Jennifer. The three-deck headline by Jennifer read:

FIND THIS COW!
$100 REWARD!
NO QUESTIONS ASKED!

In the lower-left corner was a box with summaries of stories on inside pages, including "Halloween Safety Tips" and the tryout schedule for the Say No to Drugs Community Players.

They were exhausted and didn't finish until Sunday night. Whatever could go wrong went wrong. The software for laying out pages was not that EZ; Adam had to call the company's 1-800 help line seventeen times.

Still, they did it. At 9:47 P.M. Adam popped out the CD and held it high. Their first issue as coeditors. All on that precious disk.

The next morning Adam's dad dropped off the disk at the print shop that had been doing the *Dash* for years. The shop made them a single copy—the page proofs—and Monday night Jennifer and Adam checked them over. The paper was six pages long and, to the coeditors, looked like a Michelangelo. They put their feet up and read every word over. They cradled each page in their hands like it was a leaf from the Gutenberg Bible, reading their favorite sentences out loud to each other. They laughed at the Herbs and once again were moved by Eddie. They kept staring at their own bylines.

Finally Adam said, "We did it."

"Done, done, done," said Jennifer.

Their only worry now was Marris. She had to approve the proofs. They'd make the changes she wanted, then take the corrected proofs to the print shop and get five hundred copies made.

Mrs. Marris once told them that she had not assigned an adult adviser to the *Dash* because she wanted it to be a true student newspaper. She told them she believed in freedom of the press, that censorship was the enemy of democracy. She explained that she might provide editing guidance, but it was their paper.

Adam did not believe it. Franky Cutty had set him straight early on. Franky said there used to be teacher advisers, but the last four had quit because Marris was such a witch to work with. He said the real reason it was called the *Dash* was that Marris dashed through the proofs with her editing pen, making sure nothing interesting ever got in the paper.

Tuesday morning on the way into the building, Adam dropped off the proofs in the main office. As usual, Mrs. Rose's head was at the front counter. "The principal was expecting this last week," Mrs. Rose's head said.

Adam stared at her. He found it impossible to concentrate on what Mrs. Rose's head said. There was something about the way she loomed down from the high counter and that round hairdo—it must have been an optical illusion—because even knowing the facts, he still could not help wondering if she was just the permed head.

"We'll call you down after Mrs. Marris has the opportunity to look it over," the permed head said.

Adam kept staring. Finally, the permed head said, "You can go." He stood frozen. "Are you all right, young man? You seem dazed."

"It's your head." Adam said. "Not your head. It's my rose, Mrs. Head. No! It's my head, Mrs. Rose. My head's still groggy; we were up late finishing the *Dash*. Your head's great."

"Move it, buster," the permed head said. "No way I'm giving you a late pass."

Third period, the voice of Mrs. Marris's secretary, Miss Esther, came over the loudspeaker telling Adam to report to the office. He was nervous. He didn't know if hearing back so quickly was good or bad.

The permed head buzzed in the coeditors, then led them past the ancient Miss Esther, who seemed to be taking a midmorning nap; apparently the exertion of calling Adam and Jennifer to the office had worn out the poor thing. They hurried down the stairs to the Bunker, where Mrs. Marris sat in her throne-like chair, the *Dash* proofs spread across her enormous desk.

She was smiling, which didn't mean a thing. "I

187

can see you two have been busy beavers," she said. "All in all, a good beginning for this editing team, and, really, I have just a few small things, a qualm or two, and one huge question mark."

Adam wasn't sure what a qualm was, but he was pretty certain it wouldn't improve his day. As for the huge question mark, he was certain what that was about.

"First," she said, "I was delighted by the 'Free Help!' story. A gem! That's what I call investigative reporting at its best. You found the story yourself, didn't need to be told to do it, and gave credit where credit was due. I applaud you. Now, if it were my paper, I'd have it at the top of page 1. What could be more important than a guide to help Tremble children on the state test? But I do respect that this is a student paper and it's your call. I would just ask that you include the full names of Mr. and Mrs. Boland when you mention their foundation."

"No problem," said Jennifer. "What is Mrs. Boland's first name?"

"Spring," said Mrs. Marris. "Spring Boland."

"Very good," said Jennifer. "So now that will read '. . . thanks to a generous grant from the Boland Foundation, funded by Spring and Sumner Boland.'"

188

Mrs. Marris beamed. "This is a story," said the principal, "that meets my test for good journalism: Does it help propel the Good Ship *Harris* forward? You bet it does!"

What Mrs. Marris said next surprised them. She liked the basketball hoop story. She actually said that. "I must applaud Tremble County," she said. "Those basketball hoops are the biggest eyesore, but I always assumed they were just another modern stupidity cluttering up daily life. I had no idea they were such a violation and that something could be done to get rid of them. Tear them all down, I say!"

She found the missing plywood cow story amusing and told them that she felt the sugarcoated smile contest was "pointed" but fair game, as were dentists in general ("money-suckers who didn't have the brains to get into medical school").

It was the Eddie the janitor story, she said, that gave her "real problems." She couldn't understand why they picked Eddie when there were so many "more worthy" people to profile. "He's a janitor," she said. "And we have all these educated people. Do you really want to make him a page 1 janitor?"

They were too surprised to answer.

"Don't get me wrong," Mrs. Marris continued.

"I think it's great to celebrate someone from his culture. As you know, 'Multicultural' is my middle name. No one loves Multicultural Month more than Mrs. Marris of Harris. Surely, Jennifer, you understand what I'm saying. Positive role models are so important. Now, your father, Jennifer, he's a lawyer—he's the person you ought to profile. There's a man who's done his people proud."

Jennifer's face was hot and she turned away.

Adam kept waiting for Jennifer to say something. She was so much better than he was in these tight spots. But Marris seemed to have wounded her pretty good, and when she didn't jump in, he got so nervous, so jittery, finally he just blurted out: "I love the Eddie story! It made me cry!"

For several moments there wasn't a sound in the Bunker, except the faint wheeze of Miss Esther snoring upstairs. Mrs. Marris was caught off-guard by such heartfelt honesty, a style of communication she was not accustomed to.

Finally she said, "Really?" There was a look of pure disgust on her face. "You, too, Jennifer?"

Jennifer nodded.

Mrs. Marris let out a dramatic sigh. "I would expect you, Jennifer, given your background, to understand better than anybody what I'm talking about." She paused like she was waiting for something. Then she said, "Well, you can't save people from themselves, I guess. I could not disagree more. But if you insist, I need you to take this out." And she walked around the desk and showed them what she'd circled in red:

> His newest project is building Mrs. Marris
> a set of cabinets for an electronic system
> she's having installed in the principal's
> office. He's also remodeling her bathroom.

"But, Mrs. Marris," said Adam. "That's such nice detail. It goes to the heart of the story—Eddie knows how to care for baby birds; he can be a carpenter, electrician, plumber. He may not have much schooling, but he has so many talents."

"No," said Mrs. Marris, making the grand circle back behind her desk. "It's too much detail. Slows down a story that's already dry as dust."

"I disagree," said Adam. "I think it shows—"

"Please," said Mrs. Marris. "Take it out."

Adam said, "If you'd only let me—"

"Take it out," repeated Mrs. Marris, who was

standing by her chair now, squeezing a paperweight so tight, her knuckles were white. "I said take it out. I mean take it out. Am I speaking a foreign language? Take it out, take it out, take it out. As for what you think, Mr. Big-Shot Editor, I don't give a rat's—"

"MRS. MARRIS!" Jennifer interrupted so loudly that the principal shook her head, like someone had snapped her out of a trance.

"Mrs. Marris, I see your point," Jennifer continued. "I agree completely. It really slows the flow, does not belong in this story. Too many facts can ruin a good story. We'll take it out."

Adam felt weak, seeing someone as strong as Jennifer bullied into submission, but when he glanced her way, Jennifer did not look defeated. She looked like herself again, actually a much angrier version of herself. Adam knew that look—Jennifer was smoking. Something was up.

"One more thing," barked Mrs. Marris, who wasn't even pretending to smile now. "Where is the story about Miss Bloch's gift to Harris? I gave you the whole story. Explained everything, *A* to *Z*. Where is it?"

Adam and Jennifer gave a mumbly, long-winded

explanation about how they'd been so busy with voluntary/mandatory, Quiz Bowl Gladiators, Geography Challenge, snowflake baseball, baritone lessons, science fair abstracts, tennis, church . . .

"STOP!" yelled Mrs. Marris. "STOP BLATHERING! Now, listen and listen good. That story on Miss Bloch *must* be in next month's issue. Are you clear on that? This is not a maybe. This is not something we are going to debate. This is not something you're going to tell me you didn't have time to do because you had to go to a meeting of the Future Dentists of America Club. This is an order. Make sure it's in there and on the front page. This woman donated her money to Harris. I think she deserves at least as good treatment as the school janitor, the man we call to clean up the vomit around here. IS THAT UNDERSTOOD? AM I COMING IN LOUD AND CLEAR?"

They nodded.

"Well, good," she said, waving them away. "Be gone."

As they trudged up the concrete stairs, past Miss Esther—who had reawakened and was doing the *New York Times* Sunday crossword puzzle in ink—

Jennifer was sure she knew why Marris had ordered those two sentences cut from the Eddie story.

Adam, on the other hand, did not have a clue. He was just glad to have emerged from the Bunker alive. He'd never felt so drained. His feet were concrete; his head throbbed. Mercifully, he didn't have a baritone lesson that day; in his condition, he couldn't lift a kazoo.

Jennifer arrived home that afternoon and immediately wrote Adam a long e-mail, explaining her theory on what Mrs. Marris was up to.

Adam didn't read it. By the time swim team practice was over, the emotional and physical strains of the day had taken their toll. For the first time since he was a little boy, he fell sound asleep at the dinner table. His head just plopped down on his chest between forkfuls of mashed potatoes, and he was out. His dad cradled him in his arms, carried him upstairs, and put him to bed.

It was not a peaceful sleep. Adam tossed and turned. He woke in a daze, soaked in cold sweat, then burrowed under his covers for warmth and fell asleep again, only to have another wild, crazy, feverish dream.

It's a race again. The sun is shining, the sky is blue, and he is way out in front of everybody, gliding effortlessly around the oval track. As he enters the final turn, his fans are holding up the Dash: *"Canfield Wins! Canfield Wins!" Adam has never felt happier, but then he has a nagging feeling. How did they know he won before the race was over? What's worse, and this is not a minor thing, he seems to be falling off the track. Why is that? He leans as far as he can in the other direction, straining to stay in his lane, stretching mightily, but he cannot get himself straight. In the distance he can see the other runners, tiny now, nearing the finish line, and he's alone, in the middle of the infield. The dirt is soft, so soft, that when he makes one last try at running, he sinks. Fighting is pointless; he craves rest. Deeper and deeper into the soft, warm, rich brown dirt he goes, sinking peacefully until—he's buried. What?! There's been some mistake; he can't be dead; he's a four-pluser; surely someone made an error. He refuses to die this way. He kicks and thrashes his arms to clear off the dirt and frantically opens a tiny breathing space, but as he leans farther out, toward the cool, fresh air, he goes too far and falls, down, down,*

*down. There's a thud. He's in an enormous white
room with no windows. An old woman is sitting on a
throne, and he knows her right away. Miss Minnie
Bloch. She looks like Miss Esther, but he's sure it's
Miss Bloch. And she says to him, "I'm rich. Come see
my bathroom." She opens a door, and there is the
most dazzling bathroom he has ever laid eyes on,
including a toilet bowl as big as a swimming pool,
with water that's crystal clear and so inviting. Several
swim team members are laughing and waving and
calling for him to jump in the toilet.*

Adam sat bolt upright. He was on the floor, having fallen out of bed, but his brain was wide awake.
Marris had used Miss Bloch's hard-earned money to
remodel the bathroom in the Bunker! To build custom-
made cabinets! To install an electronic system! She
wasn't spending a cent of the seventy-five thousand
dollars on kids. It was right there under their noses,
right in the Eddie story. No wonder Marris wanted
those sentences cut out. No wonder she wanted
to dump the whole Eddie article! Blessed Phoebe,
world's greatest third-grade reporter, she was
absolutely right—she had made friends with the
best source in the entire school, the man who saw

196

everything yet moved invisibly among them. Mr. Eddie James.

Adam needed to tell somebody, but it was past midnight, and of course there was only one person to tell. She'd be impressed. He slipped downstairs to the playroom and signed onto the computer. He would send Jennifer an e-mail laying out the whole thing. He glanced at his in-basket and saw a half-dozen e-mails, mostly jokes from his soccer buds.

But there was one from Jennifer, marked "urgent." He opened it. The message was really long. Adam read.

It was all there. Every last loose end tied up. Was he impressed. What a girl. She'd figured it out her-self. He checked the time it was sent—late after-noon. Even more impressive. She figured it out while she was awake. He moved the mouse, clicked the response arrow, and tapped out a brief reply so she'd see it before leaving for school the next morning:

"Good morning. You are amazing. Good night."

He slid the keyboard over and placed his head on the desk. He wasn't sleepy; his head just weighed a lot. And that's how his father found him in the morning.

chapter 13

Reader Response

Adam and Jennifer couldn't figure it out. Why didn't they feel happy? They were supposed to be on top of the world.

The *Dash* was done and heading home in the backpacks of five hundred Harris students, soon to be plopped down in the living rooms of five hundred very influential Tremble families. These were high-achieving moms and dads—lawyers, doctors, business executives—who liked to think that they were totally involved in their kids' lives and saved every scrap of paper from their schools. For years

Adam had been amazed that wherever he visited in Tremble, there was the *Dash*, hanging by a magnet on people's refrigerator doors. In technical publishing terms, the *Dash* had a long shelf life and great demographics. Or as Danny once said to Adam, "Kid, a lot of big shots read your paper."

And yet Adam and Jennifer felt like total failures. The two had worked so hard for so long, they had expected people to immediately call up and say this was the best newspaper in the history of the world.

And that did not happen.

Every single reporter was mad at them. The headlines on the stories were terrible; the play was lousy ("Why wasn't *my* story at the top of page one?"); all the best lines had been cut out.

Adam and Jennifer knew they shouldn't take this personally—good reporters were happiest when completely miserable—but even Front-Page Phoebe was bellyaching. She sent Jennifer an e-mail saying she'd worked so hard to do the smile story with some subtlety, slyly poking fun without being too mean. But then she saw the big "Sugarcoated" headline and the blown-up photo of Suzy Mollar inside the M&M bag—were Jennifer and Adam trying to make everything as cheesy as possible? Didn't they understand how upset that Phyllis woman was going to be? Worse yet, they had "totally ruined" the Eddie story by cutting out two sentences—without consulting her. "I thought you were different," Phoebe wrote Jennifer, "but, no, you're just like all big kids—nice to third graders one minute, leaving them to rot to death the next."

Adam and Jennifer had bigger problems—editor problems—that mere reporters could never fathom. They had been frightened by their meeting with Mrs. Marris in ways they couldn't even explain to each other. The two had experienced a rare peek behind the Marris smile, and though they always knew she was a phony, it was chilling to glimpse the monster lurking below.

For Jennifer, it was even more confusing, the way Marris had singled her out. Could Marris be right? Was the Eddie story embarrassing? Were there special things about being black that Jennifer was supposed to know but didn't? Her father was always making her read books about famous black Americans, so she'd know how hard it had been. Had growing up in Tremble made her too soft? Would her mom and dad be ashamed?

Having witnessed Marris's raw power close up, the editors wondered how they would ever get the Spotlight Team's cafeteria investigation into the November issue. What would they tell Sammy? He had spent a week on the computer constructing a graphic comparing stickability of a dozen mashed potato samples.

And worse than all the others combined was the Miss Bloch mess.

What were they supposed to do, ask Marris for permission to print a story saying she stole seventy-five thousand dollars of the students' money?

The October issue hadn't been read by a soul yet, and already Adam and Jennifer were certain they were doomed.

By tradition, Mrs. Marris got the first ten copies. After confirming that her editing orders had been followed, she circled the "Free Help!" story in red, underlining the sentence about the Boland Foundation's generous gift. Then she took a piece of her favorite stationery with the little bunnies dancing around the border and penned Mrs. Boland a note:

Spring:

Thought you and Sumner would like to see the latest issue of Harris's award-winning Dash! You made the front page! I can't thank you enough for all you do for our school and for Tremble! You are so beloved by the people of this great county! Bolandvision is Tremble's vision of the future! I know you humbly regard yourselves as just Spring and Sumner, but to us, you are the couple for all seasons!

Warmest regards,

and she signed her name, dotting the *i* in *Marris* with a fat little heart.

It took a few days, but just when Adam and Jennifer had abandoned all hope, they began to hear from readers. Sammy said his mom was stunned. He said usually she skimmed the paper looking for one interesting fact—like a teacher whose last name had changed because she got a divorce. Sammy's mom had been expecting a front page of Halloween safety tips and could not believe that the most interesting news was at the top of page 1, in the first paragraph, where it belonged.

One morning that week, Eddie Roosevelt James waited for Phoebe in front of the school. He told her he brought the story home and showed his wife, who showed it to their children, and they all cried. There were even things in there Eddie's grown children did not know. Mrs. James baked a batch of Toll House cookies as a thank-you, and Jennifer—Miss Journalism Ethics—said it was OK to eat them, since the story was already published and Phoebe was no longer in danger of having her reporting principles corrupted by a free cookie bribe. The entire *Dash* staff cheered Jennifer's ruling by making burping noises and polishing off Mrs. James's cookies in two minutes.

When the Harris PTA tri-presidents read the Eddie story, they decided his contribution to the school had been overlooked too long. They made a plan to hold an Eddie the Janitor Appreciation Night honoring his more than twenty-five years of service, a surprise party to be held in late November. Jennifer's mom was a big PTA honcho and filled Jennifer in.

But all Jennifer asked was, "What did Mrs. Marris say?"

Her mother gave her a long look. "Funny you should ask," said her mom. "We expected her to be excited, but she actually seemed bothered. So the PTA told her not to worry, that we'd do the whole thing ourselves, that it will come out of *our* budget, that we knew how busy she was, and all she had to do was show up and sing Eddie's praises."

"And what did she say?" asked Jennifer.

"She smiled," said her mother.

Jennifer knew that didn't mean a thing, but let it go. She was relieved by how much her mom and dad had complimented the Eddie story.

Still, Jennifer didn't talk to them or Adam or anyone about the fears Marris had planted in her mind. She was glad to put it behind her.

The great reaction to the Eddie story gave Adam and Jennifer confidence in their editing instincts. It *was* a good story; Marris was wrong. They heard compliments from kids, teachers—even adults they didn't know.

Mr. Brooks handed Adam a note, saying that in all his years at Harris, he had never read such an impressive issue of the *Dash*.

Adam's friend Danny took time from a busy day of dog and cat placements to shoot Adam an e-mail saying how amazed he was to see that real journalism was still alive in Tremble.

Even Phoebe sent Jennifer a follow-up e-mail, saying maybe she'd overreacted a tiny bit. This second e-mail was spurred by Phoebe's newfound fame. Teachers and parents were calling her a superstar, saying they couldn't remember the last time a third grader had two front-page stories. Jennifer's twin sisters reported that Phoebe was telling everyone at recess about this middle-school boy named Adam, "a really, really tough kid," who always calls her Front-Page Phoebe.

Phoebe ended her e-mail to Jennifer by saying: "This has helped me remember why I chose a career in journalism in the first place."

Not all adults were pleased.

As expected, Phyllis called to complain about the smile contest coverage. She learned about it at the Tremble Dental Association Halloween Ball. Phyllis had gone as Queen Toothpaste, complete with a red twist-on fez cap; her husband was King Floss, wrapped head to toe in white kite string. A dentist dressed as a Novocain needle had bowed dramatically to the king and queen, but later, over a scotch and soda, mentioned having a child at Harris and added how sorry he was to read what a "total disaster" the smile contest was.

People at the ball said Phyllis looked like all the paste had been squeezed from her tube.

Next morning she left a ten-minute rant on the *Dash*'s answering machine. She said that the article was all lies—though she hadn't actually read it, nor did she intend to. She complained that the little weasel of a midget reporter had twisted everything around, after Phyllis had put all her trust in that stupid flea, had given the pip-squeak all the time she needed, answered every puny question, and this was how Phyllis was paid back.

"I knew that girl was a moron dwarf, and I made the mistake of feeling sorry for the runt and helping her out," Phyllis bellowed into the phone during one of her calmer moments. She demanded a complete retraction and insisted that the reporter call back immediately.

Adam was the first to replay her call and initially was worried, but the more he listened, the more he realized that this Phyllis was a cavalcade of misinformation. Even so, he explained to Phoebe that to be fair, she had to phone Phyllis back—send her the story if she had any interest in reading it—and listen to her complaints. Then the coeditors would discuss whether there was merit to what Phyllis said or perhaps offer her the chance to write a letter to the editor.

When Phoebe heard Phyllis's voice mail, any feelings of guilt vanished. She told Adam that if she had realized Phyllis's true witchiness, she would have put even more candy in the story. Phoebe called Phyllis twice, but the charming one never returned the calls.

Within hours after the *Dash* appeared, Code Enforcement got its first call about the plan to take down all the hoops.

"You want to file a complaint, honey?" the Code Enforcement woman said to the caller. "Now, please, don't shout, please, honey. Shouting never helped anything. . . . Oooooh . . . Neither did nasty words. . . . Hold on, I'm going to walk to the next office and consult a supervisor."

She put her hand over the phone, swiveled her chair around so she was facing the Herbs, and said, "Complaint. Line 1." Instantly the Herbs put down their cheese Danishes. It was strict policy, coming straight from the top of county government—complaints had to be addressed immediately. Complaints that were ignored had a nasty tendency of finding their way up the ladder until they reached the politicians who ran the county government. And that was the last thing the politicians wanted, angry voters screaming that no one had the decency to get back to them about their complaints. It didn't take long for a bunch of unanswered complaints to pile up, and before anyone knew it, a fellow could get voted out of office and have to get a real job.

Which is not to say that the Herbs were expected to do anything about complaints beyond listen, take down the names, and promise to get back to the callers. The hope was that by letting complainers vent, they would get it out of their systems and go away. Then the politicians could continue doing whatever they darn well pleased—mostly getting their relatives county jobs that paid a nice salary, weren't hard, and didn't take lots of brains.

"That caller say what the complaint was?" asked Herb Green.

"Basketball hoops."

The Herbs looked at each other. "How would anyone know we had something going with basketball hoops?" said Herb Black.

"Caller said he read it in his kid's school paper, the *Rash.*"

Herb Green rubbed his belly, which was making rumbly noises. That second Danish had been a mistake. "Herb, you think those two kids selling Girl Scout cookies really wrote that up?"

"Don't know, Herb," said Herb Black. "You think Mrs. Boland gave them permission?"

"People would have found out anyway, once we started red-tagging the hoops, Herb," said Herb Green.

"True, Herb," said Herb Black. "But when Mrs. Boland's on a beautification kick, she's not big on giving a lot of advance warning to John Q. Public."

"Herb, you think we should call Mrs. Boland?" asked Herb Green.

Herb Black whistled. "I don't know, Herb. My philosophy on that—if it ain't broke, don't fix it."

"Right," said Herb Green. "But does that mean we should call?"

"I wouldn't," said Herb Black. "We've had one complaint; in a few days, it could all blow over. Mrs. Boland's not the kind you want to get worked up if you don't have to."

Turned out the Herbs did not have to call Mrs. Boland. She called them. By week's end the Herbs had received 187 complaints and climbing; each day they'd received more than the day before. First it was parents of Harris kids. Then those parents copied the article and gave it to parents from other parts of the county. Coaches gave it to coaches, scout leaders to scout leaders, first cousins to second cousins.

People were so upset, they didn't stop at Code Enforcement; some even called the county zoning board. Mrs. Boland's secretary had fielded a dozen complaints herself.

Mrs. Boland, of course, was one of the few people lucky enough to have an original copy of the *Dash*, thanks to Mrs. Marris. Mrs. Boland had glanced at the "Free Help!" story the Harris principal had circled, but before she could bask in that glory, she was startled to see "Your Hoop's Coming Down!" at the top of the page. Spring Boland immediately called the Herbs to ask why in the world they'd spilled the beans to a ridiculous school paper.

"We told them they should get your permission for a story," said Herb Green.

"Idiots," screamed Mrs. Boland. "Reporters don't have to ask permission."

"Those nice ones at Cable News 12 always ask," said Herb Green.

"Well, of course — we own them," said Mrs. Boland. "My Sumner always insists on hiring good-looking reporters with nice manners and tasteful clothes."

"Mrs. Boland," said Herb Black. "We're here to serve you. Tell us what to do. You want us to start red-tagging illegal hoops, or you think we should pull back and wait for this to die down?"

Spring Boland was quiet. A hard question. It might be good to back off, let people forget, and have the Herbs go after the hoops later. Mrs. Boland was a firm believer that the public was pretty stupid and would forget almost everything, including their own names, if you gave them time.

But there was a principle at stake. Mrs. Boland believed in an iron fist when it came to zoning. That was the reason she'd asked her dear husband to get her appointed to the zoning board in the first place—she didn't want Tremble turning into a slum. Someone had to keep up standards. Tremble might be one of the richest suburbs in the Tri-River Region, but as far as Mrs. Boland was concerned, it still had far too many homes with aluminum siding, chain-link fences, and aboveground pools. And those tiny shotgun houses in the Willows? What were people thinking? Why would anyone want to live like that? She envisioned a major beautification push; she wanted the county to buy all those nasty little houses, tear them down, and arrange for a builder to put up mini-estates on half-acre lots. One of the five real estate companies her Sumner owned had already bought a few of those horrible places and boarded them up, but at this rate, Mrs. Boland feared it could take years to tear down the Willows.

Basketball hoops were a perfect starting point for her master plan. And the best thing was, they were totally against the law, a blatant violation of 200-52.7A.

They had become an obsession; once she started

noticing them, she couldn't stop seeing the rusty, weathered monstrosities everywhere. Some fiberglass, some plastic, some wood, some metal; all in all, a mishmash of bad taste. Kids belonged on playgrounds, off the streets, safe and out of view. She had tried explaining this to that bothersome family living down the road from her West Tremble estate. Actually, *she* hadn't explained it to them — she'd sent her caretaker. This family was one of those large, noisy, sticky-looking assemblages — four children — with a portable hoop out front and kids playing most of the weekend and weekdays after school with their friends. Sometimes there were a dozen juveniles on the street, their bikes, scooters, and skateboards sprawled on the sidewalk, and Mrs. Boland could barely navigate her four-ton Ford Excursion past them. When Mrs. Boland's caretaker had politely suggested the playground idea to the sticky children's mother, the woman had become quite agitated. Her exact words, as reported by the caretaker, were: "Tell that Boland woman to drop dead."

Whenever she thought about that, Mrs. Boland wanted to rip down every last illegal hoop with her bare hands.

"Mrs. Boland?" said Herb Green into the phone, interrupting her thoughts. "Mrs. Boland? You still there? You want to give us any direction on this accessory structure situation?"

Did she ever. They were going on the offensive. There would be a major public campaign. They had the law on their side. "Boys!" she yelled. "Red-tag every last one of those freakin' hoops!"

She hung up and called Mrs. Marris at Harris. "Marris!" she barked, and then reamed out the principal for letting the basketball story into the paper. Nor did she get any nicer when Mrs. Marris explained that she, too, thought every hoop should be torn down. "Marris, don't you try to butterball me up," said Mrs. Boland. "If you can't control those little monsters, we can find another Harris principal mighty fast." And she slammed down the phone.

The following week, Adam was channel surfing when he caught a report on Cable News 12. The anchor said it was the first in a ten-part series, "Zoning Violations: The Silent Scourge." The one minute and forty-five second report consisted of Peter Friendly and a cameraman walking around poor neighborhoods in the Tri-River's three big cities, showing knocked-over garbage cans, dilapidated chainlink fences, stray dogs, and boarded-up aluminum-sided houses.

To provide some perspective on the Silent Scourge, Peter Friendly had interviewed Mrs. Boland.

The report ended with an ominous warning to viewers at home: "This is what happens when zoning laws are not enforced. I'm Peter Friendly, with another exclusive investigative report from Cable News 12."

Adam caught several installments—Mrs. Boland was in every one—but there was never a mention of a basketball hoop.

That month's *Dash* had one other big impact. On a Saturday in late October, after Jennifer got home from basketball practice, but before she left for a cello lesson, the phone rang. Of course, one of the twins grabbed it—they hogged everything.

It was some grownup lady for Jennifer.

"Would this be Jennifer, the journalistic savant?" said the woman.

"I'm not sure," said Jennifer.

"Well, I'm just calling to convey my gratitude," said the woman. "Thanks to you, I have my cow back." The lady on Breckenridge Road. The plywood cow! It had been returned.

"Do you have time for this, darling? You'll enjoy it," said the woman. "A few days after the *Dash* appeared, a man called the house while I was having my evening cocktail. Very mysterious conversation, reminded me of one of those pivotal moments in an Agatha Christie novel. The caller said he wished to remain anonymous. How delicious is that? He said he had overheard two boys talking about *the cow.* He gave me a phone number and a few useful tips on where it might be stashed."

Jennifer grabbed the only thing handy, a pile of napkins and a Magic Marker, and started scribbling. "OK to take a few notes?" she asked.

"Be my guest," said the woman. "So I dialed the number and a man answered. He said he didn't know anything about a cow. I asked, 'Do you think it might possibly be in your son's room?' The man said, 'I don't know. I'll get back to you.' I was surprised. He didn't seem at all upset by my insinuation."

"You didn't call the police?" asked Jennifer.

"Oh no," said the woman. "I always prefer back channels whenever possible. The intrigue is so superior. Well, the next day the man called back, said his teenagers would be by that afternoon with the cow. Sure enough, a few hours later, two young swells in a sporty convertible ride up our drive with the cow in the back seat. They seemed a bit sheepish about the cow and proceeded to tell me a confusing story about getting it from a friend who wanted to remain nameless. I didn't ask questions. Of course, they lied like they breathed."

Jennifer was having trouble keeping up; it was one juicy quote after the next. She was going to use up all the napkins and maybe the tablecloth, too.

"So my question," said the woman, "is where do I send the check?"

"The check?" said Jennifer.

"The hundred-dollar reward," said the woman. "I certainly am not going to give it to those hooligans in the convertible. You're the one who got my cow back."

"Ohhhh," Jennifer moaned.

"What is it, my dear?"

"I can't," said Jennifer. "It would be like paying the newspaper for a story."

"Really?" said the woman.

"No offense," said Jennifer, "but if newspapers took money from people to do stories, pretty soon only the rich people would have stories."

There was silence on the line, and Jennifer was nervous. Had she offended this nice lady? It was a real pain in the butt, being Miss Journalism Ethics. Why did she always have to be the responsible one?

"Jennifer," the woman said finally, "you remember how I found you? Through your mother at the garden club? You probably don't know this—your mother's hydrangeas are legendary. But I see now, she has raised something even more extraordinary than those magnificent violet flowers. *You,* my dear! No one knows better than a rich old lady like me all the cheaty things people will do for money. It is so encouraging to know that you and the *Dash* cannot be bought. Tell me this—would it be a violation of anything to write you a check for a mail subscription to the *Dash*?"

"Oh no," said Jennifer. "That's perfectly legal. But we can only charge for postage; the paper's free."

"A deal," said the woman. "I can't remember the last time I so enjoyed a Tremble newspaper. Since that awful Boland man bought the *Citizen,* the

Gazette, the *Herald,* and the *Advertiser* and merged them into one paper, there has not been an ounce of real news in Tremble. And this should make your day — did you know that Cable News 12 is following your story? They're coming by this afternoon to do a special report on my cow."

Jennifer gathered up all the paper napkins. Some had just three or four words. She'd used most of the bag; putting them in the right order would take forever. It was worth it, though. Adam would be impressed. They could run a photo of the returned cow in the November issue. She could see the headline superimposed on the back half of the cow: "A Happy Ending!"

Sitting alone in the kitchen, a rare quiet moment on a weekend afternoon, Jennifer was hoping maybe happy endings were contagious. Maybe they'd get a happy ending for the story on Marris stealing the seventy-five thousand dollars. They sure needed one.

chapter 14

Filling Holes

They skipped lunch and ducked into 306. Adam ripped a sheet of lined paper from his science binder, and together he and Jennifer made a list of what they knew and what they still had to nail down for the Miss Bloch story. They felt certain about what had actually happened — that Marris had pocketed the seventy-five-thousand-dollar gift for her own greedy purposes. But as the two of them drew up their list, Jennifer shook her head more and more. "We don't have every bit of proof," she kept saying. "We need more sources."

They knew the gift was supposed to be for kids. In his notebook Adam had highlighted the neighbor's quote in yellow and read it out loud to Jennifer, banging his fist on the sofa for emphasis. "The money," he read, "was supposed to be used to 'generally improve the life of deserving children who do not have an easy time of it.' Those are the exact words. On the record."

Even Jennifer agreed that the neighbor was a superb source. She was Miss Bloch's only friend and was letting the *Dash* print her name.

Also very important: everything the neighbor said could be checked with the lawyer who drew up Miss Bloch's will, and Adam had the man's phone number.

So they felt sure they had enough information to write about how the money was *supposed* to be used.

As to how the money was *actually* being used — what Marris did with the loot — this was the part where things got murky and Jennifer kept mumbling, "We haven't nailed it yet."

They could find no evidence that the money had been spent on kids; Jennifer had snooped around but had not heard of one new project or scholarship that seemed to be what Miss Bloch had wanted.

They knew that Marris had twisted Miss Bloch's

words, claiming the money could be used for "general improvements."

"General improvements" was just the sort of vague phrase that could justify anything, including Marris's own new bathroom, custom shelves, and electronic equipment.

"General improvements" set off the alarm in their coeditor brains that flashed COVER-UP! COVER-UP!

"General improvements" sounded really lame.

But how to prove that the money was actually used by Marris for her own purposes? How could they *prove* those were the very same dollars Marris had spent on the Bunker projects?

To Adam, it seemed obvious. "Come on," he said, "it has to be true."

"No, it doesn't have to be true," said Jennifer. "How do we know that Marris isn't using her own money for the Bunker work or some special school fund and still hasn't decided what to do with Miss Bloch's money?"

Adam's mouth opened, but nothing came out. There were times when he just hated Jennifer the editor. She could take the tiniest hole in his reporting and blow it up until it looked like the harvest moon.

"We need Eddie the janitor," said Jennifer. "He

222

did the Bunker work—he must know where the money came from. Eddie can break this story wide open. And you know who our 'in' with Eddie is."

Jennifer jumped up. "I'll send her a note through the twins." Unfortunately, it was getting harder and harder to hook up with anyone at Harris. They were all getting busier, as impossible as that seemed. Marris had added two extra classes a week of before-school/after-school voluntary/mandatory. The principal had warned that without these extra sessions, Tremble would fall behind seven other Tri-River suburbs in the number of state test prep sessions per student per week.

"We'll meet tomorrow, before school," Jennifer called out, and disappeared out the door.

Adam sunk back into the couch. He was envisioning how bad he was going to feel asking Phoebe for a favor.

After school Adam leafed through his notebook and found the phone number for the lawyer who had drawn up Miss Bloch's will. The law firm had an office in downtown Tremble, over a bank. Adam explained to the woman who answered the phone

223

that he was a reporter for the *Dash* and then asked to speak to the lawyer.

"Sorry," said the woman. "He's deceased."

"Wow," said Adam. "How diseased is he?"

"Deceased," said the woman. "He's totally deceased."

"Whoa," said Adam. "Anyone totally diseased must be totally contagious. Is it safe for me to talk to him on the phone?"

"Not diseased. D-E-C-E-A-S-E-D," spelled the woman. "I should have known better than trying to be subtle with a newspaper reporter. He is completely and irrevocably stone-cold D-E-A-D. Is that a word you can spell?"

Adam gasped. "Oh, my gosh," he said. "I am so sorry. I feel like an idiot."

"Well," said the woman. "You sound like an idiot. What rag did you say you're from?"

"The *Dash*," said Adam.

"Never heard of it," said the woman. "That another Boland publication?"

"Oh no, ma'am, nobody owns us," said Adam. "We're the student newspaper of Harris Elementary-Middle."

The woman was quiet, then softly said, "My

word. The paper that did the basketball hoop story? What's your name?"

"Adam Canfield."

"Adam Canfield of the *Dash!*" she said. "I can't believe it's you. Every lawyer in this office was talking about your basketball story. We got five new clients thanks to you. They've hired our zoning specialist to fight that accessory structure nonsense."

"Really?" said Adam.

"Really," said the woman. "Tell me, how can I help you, sweetheart?"

Adam explained about the Minnie Bloch story and how he was hoping to verify the gift she left to Harris.

"Well, the lawyer may be dead," she said, "but the will is public record. All wills are in this state. You can get a copy at the county courthouse in the probate office."

Adam didn't say anything; he was thinking about taking three buses to the courthouse. He was thinking he would never get to play another game of manhunt for as long as he lived.

"We might have a copy here," she continued, "if the will was filed in the last two years, we'd still have it. Like me to check?"

She put down the phone. When she returned,

she said, "Your lucky day. I'll make a copy and mail it to you. Normally we charge a dollar a page, but since it's for the *Dash*," she said, "I'll do it for free."

Adam was excited.

"Now I want something in return," she said. "Can you get me a mail subscription?"

Oh, could he. Before hanging up, he thanked her a million times.

"No," she said, "I should thank you. Truth is a mighty precious commodity. Adam Canfield of the *Dash*, you keep up the good work, you hear?"

He couldn't wait to tell Jennifer, but she didn't stop by 306 that afternoon.

When he got home, he went into the garage and grabbed his basketball. He needed to practice foul shots. His coach had told them that many a game was won or lost at the free-throw line. Coach said they ought to be making six of ten every time. Coach said there were no shortcuts, just lots of hard work.

The wind was harsh off the river, and his hands turned red and ached after a few minutes, but he needed to be out there. He pulled his sweatshirt hood over his head, taking several shots from the outside to warm up. And then he noticed. There, on the beam that supported the backboard, was a red sticker, about three inches square. He assumed some kid had put it there. Once when he'd ridden his bike to school, he'd come out and found a sticker on the seat that said, *In case of nuclear attack, stick your head between your legs and kiss your butt goodbye.*

But this sticker was no joke.

It said:

N O T I C E !
STRUCTURE VIOLATES LOCAL ORD. 200-52.7A.
REMOVE AT ONCE!
YOU HAVE 7 DAYS!
NONCOMPLIANCE MAY RESULT IN $500 FINE

PER DAY AND IMMEDIATE REMOVAL PER ORDER OF

TREMBLE COUNTY ZONING BOARD.

Adam had been red-tagged.

chapter 15

Two Secret Sources

Adam, Jennifer, and Phoebe met so early the next morning, three of their six eyeballs still had sleepy bugs. The school wasn't open yet, so they walked to the West River Diner, where they took seats in the rear. Jennifer had once read in a biography of Thomas Dewey that when great investigators eat in a restaurant, they sit with their backs to the rear wall so no one can sneak up from behind and shoot them.

The waitress was upset because they had taken a booth during the morning rush and just ordered hot chocolates. But the three news hounds did not notice; they were all business.

In voices barely above a whisper, the coeditors gave Phoebe the high points of the Miss Bloch story.

"You mean you're going to write an article saying Mrs. Marris is a common low-down crook?" asked Phoebe.

"Shhhhhh," they shushed her.

"Whoa," said Phoebe. "Not a bad little story. That'll probably make the front page, huh?"

"Probably," said Adam, "if we live to tell it." They explained that they needed to talk to Eddie to see where Marris got the money for the Bunker work.

"Wait until you see the bathroom," said Phoebe. "It has gold handles on everything. It's got a sauna. It's got this weird thing Eddie said they have in Europe, I can't remember the name, something like a biddy—rich people use them to wash their . . ."

"You saw the bathroom?" asked Adam. "Gold fixtures?"

"Sure," said Phoebe. "Eddie showed me when I followed him around—it was my fourth or fifth interview. After everyone was gone, he took me to the Bunker to see the work he was doing."

"So you think you can get Eddie to talk with us?" asked Adam.

"No problem," said Phoebe. "Eddie's my guy.

He'll do what I ask. We are so tight." She paused. "You know, I was just thinking—I was right about Eddie, wasn't I? Did I say he was the guy who knew everything at Harris? Remember that day when you yelled at me?"

"Yeah, yeah," said Adam.

"Remember, you said Eddie was going to be so boring?"

"Yeah, yeah," said Adam.

"And you told me—"

"PHOEBE," yelled Adam. "I give up; I surrender. You were right; I was wrong. You are king of the universe and I am a blackhead on the butt of a lowly warthog. Once again, you have proved—"

"Easy," said Jennifer. "Let's calm down . . . Phoebe, we know how much you've done and we really appreciate it."

Phoebe nodded. She had done a lot. She said she would help them on one condition—that she got a byline on the Marris story, too.

"No problem," said Adam. "If you want, we'll put just your byline on it all by itself."

"Really?" said Phoebe.

"He's kidding," said Jennifer. "We would never do that to you." It was almost time for the first bell

230

and they stood to leave. "See you after school?" said Jennifer.

"Be there or be square," said Phoebe.

She spotted Eddie at recess, by the Dumpster. When she explained that the *Dash* editors wanted to speak with him, he seemed pleased, until he heard what it was about, and then he was plainly nervous and edgy.

"I don't know, Phoebe," he said. "You know how grateful I been, I'd do anything to help, but you are dealing with dynamite on this one."

"Come on, Eddie," joked Phoebe. "Relax. What's the worst Marris could do?"

"Child, don't be ignorant," snapped Eddie. His voice was so different, Phoebe felt a shiver race through her. "You don't know how deep this lady's hate goes," he said. "Don't be fooled by her happy-face smiles. If Marris knew I was telling her secrets, she would fire me in a second. That witch would do anything to save her white behind."

Phoebe was speechless. Was this the same Eddie? She had been so sure she could deliver him for her coeditors. How did things go wrong so fast?

She couldn't think. Was there some way that a

reporter persuades people to talk, even when talking will get them into trouble?

She was sure that real grown-up reporters must have special techniques—maybe secret words—for getting people to spill their guts. But nothing came to her. Worse yet, she wasn't sure she wanted to change Eddie's mind. She couldn't bear to hurt Eddie. He was so angry at her now. She wanted the old Eddie back.

Recess was almost over. On the other side of the playground, kids were lining up to file back into the building. They looked so happy. Phoebe couldn't imagine why anyone would want to be a reporter. It was the perfect job for a pit viper.

Eddie didn't say another word, and when he turned to dump a barrel of old planks into the Dumpster, Phoebe ran away as fast as her little legs would go.

After school, she peeked through the windowpane in the door to 306. Jennifer and Adam were waiting for her. They were laughing about something. Probably one of their annoying middle-school inside jokes. Phoebe didn't want to go in. How was she going to tell them that Eddie wouldn't talk? Adam would start screaming again.

She turned to walk away, but Jennifer spotted her, jumped up, and led her into the room.

"So, Front-Page," said Jennifer. "When do we see Eddie?"

Phoebe said nothing, stared at the floor.

"This afternoon?" said Adam. "We've really got a lot of stuff to tie together here." Adam had been working on a list of questions.

Phoebe still didn't say anything.

"He is going to talk to us?" asked Adam.

Phoebe did not lift her head.

"Whoa," said Adam. "Eddie's your guy, right? He'll do whatever you ask, right? You two are as tight as ticks, right? Are you telling me—"

"Stop it, Adam," said Jennifer.

"Two peas in a pod was my understanding," said Adam. "Tweedledum and Tweedledee."

"Stop it, Adam," repeated Jennifer.

"Oh geez," said Adam, finally noticing the tears rolling down Front-Page's cheeks. "I didn't mean— I'm sorry, Phoebe, I am, it's just—we're under so much pressure."

Jennifer pulled a tissue from her backpack and handed it to Phoebe.

"I asked him," Phoebe said finally, explaining how Eddie had turned her down because he feared Marris. "I felt terrible," Phoebe said, "like I forgot to think about Eddie's feelings. Like I'd betrayed a friend for some stupid story. Like I was just thinking of front-page glory."

Adam and Jennifer were quiet. They knew the feeling. Every good reporter does. Finally Jennifer said, "How about this. What if we talk to Eddie but don't use his name?"

They looked at each other. "That's good," said Adam.

"Wait," Phoebe said to Adam. "Weren't you the one who gave me this big lecture on how we have to use names, how using real names holds us to a higher standard. You were the one who said I had to let the whole world know that the dental association's biggest idiot was Phyllis Cooper—spelled C-O-O-P-E-R. Remember how we're not supposed to worry about hurt feelings? Our job is to tell the truth, no matter what, blah, blah, blah."

Adam sneaked a peek at Jennifer. He didn't

know how to answer that. Phoebe really thought fast for third grade.

"I see your point," said Jennifer, "but this is different."

Dental society members, Jennifer said, had been looking for publicity. They had issued press releases, wanted to promote their cause and make themselves look like public heroes. They were fair game. "In this case," she said, "we're going to Eddie, he's getting nothing out of this, and we could be putting him in real danger by using his name."

"You sure?" said Phoebe.

Jennifer hesitated. "Pretty sure," she said.

"Pretty sure?" said Phoebe.

"You know, Phoebe," said Jennifer, "I might look like a big middle schooler who's got all her ducks in order, but I'm going to let you in on something. I'm just doing my best here, trying to figure out this stuff as we go."

Adam tried to get Jennifer's attention, but she was totally focused on Phoebe. Jennifer really wowed him sometimes. How did she know to say that stuff?

Phoebe nodded. "OK," she said. "It happens I agree."

"Good," said Jennifer. "So we'll try talking to Eddie just for background, no name, then maybe he can lead us to people who can have their names printed in the *Dash*. This is great—we have a plan."

But Phoebe was not finished. "What about your coeditor," she said, refusing to even look in Adam's direction. "Are you sure this is OK with your coeditor? Because way back at the first *Dash* meeting this year, when I said the stuff about Eddie was hush-hush, your coeditor screamed at me for being a Secret Agent Phoebe."

Both girls stared at Adam, who looked embarrassed.

"You know, Phoebe," he said softly. "I don't like to admit this too much, but sometimes when I get worked up, I yell stuff—I don't know what I'm talking about."

He felt like an idiot, telling his deepest secrets to a third grader. But then he caught a glimpse of Jennifer smiling at him, and there was a small, sensational burst of joy in Adam's chest.

They took turns peeking out the *Dash*'s third-floor windows to see if the car was gone yet. While they

236

were waiting, Adam figured he'd get his twenty minutes of practicing done now so he'd have one less thing to do at home; then he might actually have a shot at being in bed by 11:30. He pulled out his baritone and played "Sweet Betsy," the Level II piece he was doing for the statewide music competition. If he scored high enough—at least twenty-six of twenty-eight points—he might make the honors band.

Finally, a little before five o'clock, Jennifer spotted Marris leaving with Miss Esther. The principal had her arm under the old woman's elbow and was guiding her down the front stairs. Miss Esther was so bent over, her chin nearly touched her knees. Jennifer felt sad watching them. She had to give Marris credit for keeping Miss Esther in a job. Jennifer felt uneasy. Were they being too harsh on Marris? Marris's concern for Miss Esther was impressive, considering how totally useless the poor old bat was. What if Marris really was a decent human being?

After gently helping Miss Esther into the passenger side, Mrs. Marris climbed behind the wheel, gunned the engine, and screeched off, leaving rubber. In seconds her red Porsche was gone.

*   *   *

The boiler room was pleasantly warm on this chilly November afternoon. The heat from the ceiling pipes and the steady hum of the oil burner made it a cozy spot.

But Eddie looked cold as ice, even after Phoebe explained that they had no intention of using his name. He gave them three milk crates to sit on but remained standing. "So this is off the cuff?" said Eddie.

"You mean, off the record?" said Adam.

"Listen, young man, I don't know the fancy words, but I will tell you this, if Marris finds out I talked to you, I will lose my job. I have children in college I got to support. I got my wife's mother on disability living with us. How many good-paying jobs you know for black folks my age with no education? What you are up to is no game. You are talking about this lady stealing the public's money. People go to jail for that."

Adam and Jennifer knew this but had never said it out loud, even to each other. It sounded scary coming from someone else, dangerous. Once again, it occurred to them that they were out of their minds.

"What makes you think you can even get this in

your paper?" Eddie continued. "You think Marris will let you print her death notice? Suppose I tell you what I know and she don't let you print it? What do you think will happen to me? Do you know how she lit into me after Phoebe here's story? She wanted to know why I'm telling that little brat—no offense, Phoebe, her words, not mine—about the work I done in the Bunker. She says to me, 'Eddie you know, even a fish wouldn't get caught if it kept its mouth shut.'"

"If this comes to my word against Marris, who you think people will believe?" said Eddie. "Not the man in the boiler room, that's who."

Jennifer wasn't so sure. With Eddie the Janitor Appreciation Night fast approaching, all kinds of people would soon be making speeches about how great he was—even Marris, with a little luck. And Phoebe would be right there taking down all those terrific quotes about Eddie. That would make him look like a mighty strong source when the story about Miss Bloch's gift came out.

The problem was, of course, they couldn't tell Eddie. It would ruin the surprise party.

"Mr. James," said Jennifer. "Suppose you tell us

what you know. Then at the end, we'll go back and see if there might be some information we could use and no one would know it was from you."

"There won't be," said Eddie.

"If there isn't," said Jennifer, "that's that. It is one hundred percent your call."

As Adam went through his questions, he realized there was so much they knew that Eddie didn't. Eddie didn't know the gift was supposed to be for kids; he didn't know the amount of the gift; he didn't know anything about Miss Bloch except her name. It made Adam realize—he and Jennifer really had found out a lot on their own. They were the only ones to take the time to fit together all the pieces to this puzzle.

The reporters asked if Eddie had any idea how much the work had cost so far.

"Nope," said Eddie. "But I could add it up. I got all the work-order slips."

Work-order slips? The reporters looked confused.

"Any time I do a special project that costs more than two thousand dollars, they have to give me a special work-order slip. That's strict board of education rules. Written in the law. On this one, I got special order slips for all the new plumbing, the wood cabinets, the electronic equipment."

"You keep those slips, Eddie?" asked Adam.

"You know I do," he said. "I got a copy of every special order slip since I come on this job twenty-seven years ago. Man's got to protect himself when swimming in shark-infested waters."

Jennifer thought of a little trick she'd learned from listening to a Sunday news show on National Public Radio. "Mr. James," she said, "I realize you don't know how much all this cost, but would you guess it's more than five thousand dollars? Just guess. We're not quoting you on it."

"Honey, you won't be quoting me on any of this."

"Right, right," said Jennifer.

"Way more than five thousand," said Eddie.

"More than twenty-five thousand?" asked Jennifer.

"Oh yeah," said Eddie. "I'd say so far we're in the fifties, and we ain't done. I just put in a new order for twenty-five security cameras."

"'In the fifties'—you mean more than fifty thousand dollars?" asked Adam.

"Absolutely," said Eddie. "Those gold faucets,

gold shower heads, gold door handles—they add up mighty fast."

They wanted to know what those special order slips said. Did they mention the gold plumbing?

"Marris is no fool," said Eddie. "She writes it in fancy words that don't say nothing." And here Eddie did his imitation—which was actually quite good—of a snob saying, "Plumbing expenditures, Harris construction project, phase one."

All three reporters laughed so hard, they nearly fell off their milk crates. "I didn't know you did imitations of rich ladies," said Phoebe.

"Lots you don't know about me, Phoebe," said Eddie.

Phoebe looked hurt.

"And there's lots you found out for your write-up," said Eddie. "Now, don't get broody."

Adam wanted to ask for copies of those special order slips, but he didn't know how to without getting Eddie so worked up that the three of them would get kicked out of there.

Fortunately, Jennifer was way ahead of him.

She asked Eddie how many people receive copies of those slips, which started him figuring. There was Marris and the office secretaries; there were the school district's business managers, plus their assistants; there was the district's chief custodian and his assistants.

Eddie guessed fifteen people altogether might have copies of those special order slips.

"So if you gave us copies of those slips, no one would know it came from you," said Jennifer, trying to sound matter-of-fact. "There might be fifteen different people who could have given them to us."

Eddie thought about that a long while. Then he nodded. "OK," he said. "I get what you're saying. I just hope you get how much I'm trusting you. When you write your story, every time you type a word, you think about how much harm you could cause me if you pick the wrong word."

Adam glanced at his notes. One more big question. There was a rhythm to this kind of reporting, and he'd saved the hardest question for last.

"Did you ever hear Marris actually say that it was the gift to the school that paid for the Bunker work?" asked Adam.

"Oh yeah," said Eddie. "Bunch of times. You got to remember, I'm down there a lot working."

That was it — they had Marris.

"Don't even consider it," said Eddie. "Even

without my name, she'd think of me right away. You can't be saying, 'Sources told the *Dash* this or that.' She'll see right through that 'sources' baloney. She'll know right away it's Eddie Roosevelt James."

Adam tried to look calm, but he was frantic. They needed that fact. It was the glue that held everything together. *Money that was supposed to go to kids was paying for gold plumbing in the principal's bathroom.*

How were they going to write their story without that information? Could they write the story without it? Eddie didn't want it in, even without his name.

And then Jennifer spoke. "Eddie," she said, "you ever hear Marris say to anyone else that she was using gift money for the Bunker?"

"Oh sure," said Eddie. Adam sat ramrod straight on his crate, his pen ready. Jennifer to the rescue.

Eddie named Miss Esther, Mrs. Rose, and the teacher who oversaw before-school/after-school voluntary/mandatory.

Adam's shoulders sagged. He didn't even bother taking down the names. He felt like the roller coaster he was stuck on was once again barreling downhill, out of control, leaving his stomach up in his throat. None of those people did the reporters any good.

Miss Esther and Mrs. Rose certainly weren't going to tell the *Dash* anything bad about Marris. And while Adam didn't know the teacher who ran before-school/after-school, he was sure she was a major Marris suck-up.

"Anyone else?" asked Adam. "Anyone you can think of?"

Eddie was quiet. "Yes," he said, finally. "Mr. Brooks."

"The world history teacher?" asked Adam.

Eddie nodded. "I was working on Marris's bathroom one day, start of school year. I think she forgot I was in there. That Bunker is so big, it takes forever just to walk from one side to the other. And Mr. Brooks and Marris, they're starting out, making nice chitchat. Something like he says, 'Having some work done?' And she says, 'Yes, we've had a gift for the school.' They yap about that a little, the importance of charity, yap, yap, yap. And the next thing I know, she is hollering at him at the top of her lungs about test scores. Really nasty stuff. Mean."

"Mr. Brooks doesn't like Marris," said Adam. "She ended World Domination."

"Mr. Brooks hates Marris," said Eddie.

"You know that?" asked Adam.

"Mr. Brooks and I been walking-around buds for years," said Eddie. "He's good people. I don't mind doing little extras for Mr. Brooks. He loves to teach. Loves children. You know he invited me to see that World game he played? He was so proud of it."

chapter 16

A Bad Omen

Room 306 had always been the place where Adam went when he needed to flop on a couch and joke away an afternoon, to stop everything he was doing and let the steam out of his head.

No more.

In the old days, when his only job was being a star reporter, he'd get his story done and somehow the rest of the paper came out. Now he, Adam, *was* Mr. Somehow; nothing seemed to get finished until he had worried it to death.

He knew from his dreams that he was losing his grip. They were getting stranger and stranger, which was saying a lot. In his latest, he was running on a track again, leading the race as usual. He had never heard such cheering, and just as he was beginning to enjoy the applause, he noticed they weren't yelling for him—they were laughing at him. He looked down and realized he'd forgotten his clothes; he was running stark naked—except where the fig leaf usually went, he'd been red-tagged.

Boy, did he need to air out his head. Thankfully, there was still one place where the air was plentiful and life felt easy. The next afternoon, he skipped voluntary/mandatory. They were supposed to review chapter 43 in the state test guide: how to maximize your score when there's only one minute left and you still have unanswered questions.

He rode the early bus home. Some middle-school boys gave him a hard time, saying he couldn't possibly be Adam Canfield if he was on the early bus, that the real Adam Canfield was still at school sucking up to Marris and her goons. They blocked his way to the back of the bus, where the big kids sat. Normally, Adam would have lunged past them to the rear bench seat, landing on kids' laps and causing a rumble. Today he didn't have the energy and just sat toward the front, where third and fourth graders kept sneaking curious looks at him.

At home, alone, he dropped off his backpack and baritone, grabbed a green apple, then walked down the block, to the river. It was funny—he lived so close but could go weeks without visiting the river.

The streets in Adam's neighborhood dead-ended into a walkway that ran along the Tremble for miles. Adam turned the corner and headed upriver. It was quiet, no joggers or bikers.

Adam knew that the river was many rivers. Each season it changed. In summer the river was busy and noisy, thick with pleasure boats and tourists. There were cabin cruisers and fifty-foot sailboats, many heading to the ocean. There were little Butter-flies, Sunfish, and putt-putts out for a few hours of sailing or fishing. They so crowded the river that Adam imagined he could make it from one bank to the other by stepping from boat to boat.

Not far from Adam's house, by a big bend in the river, was a town beach. It was really just a set of docks that had been lashed together and then anchored to steel posts. At one end of the docks was a diving board. Adam loved to jump in and let the current pull him to the far end of the docks, where he'd swim for the ladder, then do it all over again. Even in mid-August, the water was cool, and some days last summer Adam and Jennifer had flopped on the docks in the hot afternoon sun, chatting and snoozing until their skin was beaded with sweat. Then they'd jump up and race to be first off the diving board.

In spring, Adam rode his bike downriver and watched the crew teams from the state campus at Tremble race.

Twice in his lifetime, the winter had been cold enough for the river to freeze. He had learned to skate his third-grade winter, going out on the river with his mother night after night. After they grew weak and wobbly, he and Mom laid on their backs in the dark stillness, listening to the ice creak and searching the winter sky for shooting stars.

The river was frigid and gray in late fall, but Adam loved how quiet and powerful it felt with the tourists gone. He'd see a line of coal barges or hear the foghorn of a tug moving upriver. Fall was when Adam and Danny used to come for a skip.

Adam reached the boathouse at Long Bluff. It was a famous landmark, a big yellow wooden building jacked up high off the river to protect it from even a hundred-year flood. Sailboats tacking on the river used it as a bearing, and fishermen found their favorite spots by calculating the distance from the boathouse. It had large handsome flower boxes under the main-floor windows that the civic association members planted each spring with red geraniums and yellow marigolds. Families stored their kayaks, canoes, and small sailboats in the lower half of the building; upstairs was a large musty sitting room full of canvas chairs and wicker couches, a perfect place to watch a summer sunset.

This time of year the boathouse was boarded up for winter.

Adam followed the boardwalk that crossed over the bluff to the boathouse, then climbed down a ladder to the dock and river below.

The Tremble was low, leaving a sliver of sandy bottom and plenty of rocks exposed at the bank's edge. Adam hunted up several handfuls of flat rocks, made a pile, and began skipping them.

He was good. To get the most skips out of a rock, he used plenty of wrist and angled his body low so his arm came whipping around parallel to the water. If he stood too erect and threw with a downward motion, the rock would make one big skip, then sink.

When Adam was in the zone, he could skip a rock so many times, with each skip so close to the next, it was impossible to count them all. Danny had once said it looked like a motorboat skimming the water's surface, and the phrase stuck.

To repeatedly throw motorboats took skill, but also the right conditions — mainly flat water.

Adam threw all his rocks, gathered more, threw all those, then did it again. It felt good to throw as hard as he could and burn off his anger and worries. He'd needed a big skip. Seeing a rock do a motorboat never failed to give him a sense of satisfaction.

For a long time he skipped rocks, thinking of nothing, losing track of time. Then he noticed he was getting cold and that started his worries creeping back. He told himself if he could throw three straight motorboats, it would mean that the Miss Bloch story would turn out great and he wouldn't have to worry about Marris.

By then the wind had picked up, sending small, choppy swells in toward the bank. Repeatedly, his rock would catch a wave, pop high in the air, and sink after two or three skips. Adam never did get three motorboats in a row, and finally quit, walking home in the dark, chilled and full of worries.

Phoebe heard about it from her mother, who signed at the mall.

Jennifer's dad told her about it; he signed at the train station on the way into the city.

Danny signed in front of Pitkin's Rexall, where a little table had been set up.

The lady with the plywood cow signed by the cash register at O'Rourke Hardware.

Betty Willard signed at the Pine Street AME Zion Church in the Willows.

But it wasn't until Saturday morning that Adam found out. Their doorbell rang, a rare occurrence. Adam ignored it. He knew it wouldn't be for him. There weren't many kids on his block, and his friends usually called or instant-messaged before biking over, or they just hollered from the street.

Adam's mom got the door, was out there a little while, then came back inside. "Adam," she called, "come downstairs. I want you to hear this."

Adam took his sweet time, hitting each step harder than normal just to remind his mother that he was doing her a huge favor. On the front porch was a woman and her daughter. The girl was little, second or third grade. She had blond pigtails, was missing her two front teeth and holding a clipboard. What struck Adam most, though, was over her sweatshirt she wore a basketball T-shirt, a Bill Russell Hall of Fame jersey—not an easy item to find in the Tri-River Region.

"Go ahead, kitty," said the mother. "Start again."

"A tewwible thing is happening," said the little girl. "Bad people want to take away the little childwen's basketball hoops. What are they, cwazy? Do they want us all to get hooked on dwugs? You should wead this." She handed Adam a copy of Adam's story from the *Dash*.

Adam was practically glowing. "I've read it," he said.

"He wrote it," said his mother.

"Wrote it?" said the woman. "*This* is Adam Canfield of the *Dash*?!"

Adam tried not to glow too much.

"Kitten-witten," said the woman. "This is the young man who wrote the story about the hoops."

The girl took a moment to absorb that. "Wow,"

she said. "Can I have your autogwaph, Mr. Canfield?"

"Several youth groups in the community are circulating petitions," the woman explained. "We're going to present them to the zoning board. I don't know what those zoning people were thinking."

"Do they want us all to get hooked on dwugs?" said the little girl.

"It's OK, kitty," said the mother. "Save it. These people understand."

"Are they twying to make the little childwen misweble?" said the girl.

Adam's mom signed and called down his dad, who also signed.

"How many childwen have to die to make this cwaziness stop?" said the little girl.

"Kitty, calm down," said the mother. "You're going to wear yourself out. This is just our fourth street."

As the mother led her down the block, Adam could hear the little girl chanting, "No justice, no peace, save the childwen. No justice, no peace, save the childwen."

* * *

Peter Friendly of Bolandvision 12 was at the downtown river pier, at Huck Finn's California Sushi De-Lite, when he learned about the petition. In his loudest, most Friendly voice, he had just finished explaining to the hostess exactly who he was, which important people he knew, and what table by the window he preferred, when a man with paper and pen approached. Peter Friendly assumed it was a fan seeking an autograph and gave him his Friendly-est smile, but was surprised to learn that the fellow just wanted him to sign a basketball petition. The man explained that he coached a CYO team and said in all his years, he had never seen such a response to a petition.

Peter Friendly didn't bother calling this information in to his news director. From his ten-part groundbreaking investigation of zoning scourges, he knew the Bolands were not interested in basketball zoning stories. And besides, his table by the river was ready.

Sumner Boland never heard a word of the petition. He was an incredibly busy man, a national force, spending every waking hour cutting deals, hobnobbing with politicians, and protecting his cable monopoly in forty-eight television markets. His professional life was soaring upward at a dizzying pace. These days, stories in the *Citizen-Gazette-Herald-Advertiser* no longer referred to him as a "business-man"; he was a "telecommunications magnate." So as not to waste a moment, Mr. Boland raced about the Tri-River Region in a Bolandvision 12 helicopter. Unfortunately, private helicopter pads were one of the few places where parents circulating petitions did not set up card tables, leaving the telecommunications magnate totally disconnected on this one.

Mrs. Boland, too, was clueless. She had recently realized she was exhausted from all her zoning work. Out of her own pocket, she had hired the top advertising firm in the Tri-River Region to put together a five-minute video clip on her vision for Tremble in the next century. She planned to use it to kick off the December zoning board meeting. She told the video crew to spare no expense and suggested that for background music they use a recording of Frank Sinatra singing "My Way." With everything in place for the meeting, she realized as usual the one person she had neglected was herself and did the only thing that made sense: jetted down to Saint Kitts for two weeks of tropical sun. She wanted to look her best for the big meeting.

Herb Black and Herb Green knew all about the petitions. It seemed every time the Herbs stopped at the Marvel Ice Cream stand or the Tasty Choice doughnut shack for a little pick-me-up, someone would ask them to sign a petition.

The Herbs had stopped red-tagging hoops during daylight hours. Once word got out, people were pretty hostile. A man who caught them in the act had run out his front door, scaring the Herbs so, they had dived for cover in a neighbor's hedges. While the Herbs prayed for their lives, the man raced around their county vehicle, slapping a roll of his daughter's yellow happy-face stickers all over the car.

Later the Herbs remarked that for such happy little faces, they were an enormous pain to remove without scratching the vehicle.

Since then the Herbs had worked an 11 P.M. to 7 A.M. shift to finish all 1,048 red tags. They didn't mind; they got an extra fifty cents an hour differential for the night shift.

The closer the zoning meeting got, the more nervous the Herbs grew. Every time the phone rang, they were sure it was Mrs. Boland, but it was just another complaint from some basketball hothead.

Herb Green wondered if they ought to interrupt

258

Mrs. Boland's vacation to warn her about the petitions. "I don't know, Herb," said Herb Black. "You know my philosophy — if it ain't broke, don't fix it."

"But, you know," said Herb Green. "I think it might be broke."

"Well, Herb," said Herb Black. "You understand how Mrs. Boland has her heart set on tearing down every last hoop. She has got a major case of red-tag fever. If you want to call and tell her she's making a mistake, you go ahead. But do me a favor, Herb? Make sure, in a nice loud, clear voice, you say, 'This is Herb Green calling, not Herb Black, repeat not Herb Black.'"

Herb Green mulled that over. "You know, Herb," he finally said. "Maybe I won't call."

chapter 17

Animosus Atque Fortis Appare!

As much as Adam loved world history class, he was having trouble concentrating. It seemed no matter what the topic, no matter how ancient and far away the historic period, Adam felt like it was about him. And the omens were all rotten. Just when one of Mr. Brooks's lessons seemed headed for a happy ending, a disastrous turn of events would undo all the hopeful stuff and make Adam feel miserable about his own prospects.

They discussed how brave and noble Brutus had been to assassinate his buddy Caesar in order to preserve Rome's republic. That made Adam-Brutus feel hopeful about his epic struggle with Marris, until they got to the part about Adam-Brutus being defeated in battle, killing himself, the republic being smashed, and the dictatorship returning.

And Cleopatra—what a nightmare. Every time Cleopatra-Marris seemed about to be dethroned, she hooked up with some big shot like Augustus or Marc Antony or Sumner J. Boland and went right on ruling Egypt like her usual dastardly self.

In the unit on world explorers, Adam felt at one with Christopher Columbus, out on the open seas against all odds, showing those idiots in England, France, Portugal, and on the early bus that it really was a round world. But then they get to the part where Adam-Columbus is considered a despot by his own men, gets shipped back to Spain in chains, and dies in "poverty and neglect." Those were the exact words in the book: "poverty and neglect." What was that about? They couldn't even cook up a happy ending for Columbus? If the most famous explorer in history went down the tube, what chance did Adam have?

In his world history essay for the first-term final, Adam laid all this out in excruciating detail and more — pointing out that Virgil died before finishing the *Aeneid*, Archimedes was murdered by some idiot Roman, and Magellan did not make it around the world.

Mr. Brooks had never read a bleaker vision of world history from a Harris student, and on the day the exams were returned asked Adam to stop by after school. "It's nothing bad," Mr. Brooks said. "Your grasp of the material is superb. I just wanted to share a few thoughts."

After school the teacher gave Adam a warm welcome — *Salve, amicus!* — and motioned for him to sit. Adam flopped down in the front row.

Mr. Brooks perched himself atop a student desk across from Adam.

"You know, Adam," said Mr. Brooks, "you are one of the finest students I've taught. But I'm worried. Your essay . . . It was . . . How to put this? . . . Devoid of all hope. I was wondering, are you all right? You don't strike me as that kind of person. You always seem so full of life."

Adam shrugged and in a barely audible voice said, "It's not my fault all the great people had miserable endings."

"But not quite that miserable," said Mr. Brooks.

"Some may have fallen short of their bold dreams, but what they achieved . . ."

"And the bad people," said Adam, "they just went on and on creating mayhem and havoc."

"I grant you," said Mr. Brooks, "Cleopatra did hang on for a long time, but in the end, you mustn't forget my lecture—how the inevitability of Rome's rise caught up with her and there was that quite dramatic poison-snake-to-the-bosom finale."

Adam nodded. "One person," he mumbled.

"Not one person," said Mr. Brooks. "I don't think I'm giving away too much world history to say that if you stay tuned, you will find that Franklin Roosevelt saves the nation from the Depression and the evil Hitler, that a world government known as the United Nations gets formed and endures, and in less than a century—a millimeter on the global timeline—Russia throws off monarchy and communism and chooses democracy.

"You know," Mr. Brooks went on, "history certainly teaches us that treachery lurks around every corner. And yet, against all odds, despite every form of human stupidity, we Homo sapiens are still here."

"Yeah, right," Adam mumbled. "What about Rwanda?"

"Well, yes . . . I don't deny . . . Look, Adam, my point is I'm worried that all you're seeing is the bad. Is anything wrong?"

Adam hesitated. He didn't know if he should tell Mr. Brooks the truth. What use was it? Mr. Brooks seemed even more afraid of Marris than Adam was. That last talk they had about Marris had left Adam feeling so blue, so powerless, so embarrassed for Mr. Brooks. If Mr. Brooks didn't stand up for his own World Domination game, why would he help them on the Miss Bloch story? This man had talked so much about how important it was to preserve his dignity and privacy and his bachelor life. What was that about? Just a fancy way of saying he was afraid to lose to Marris? Adam wondered what the Latin word was for "coward."

Jennifer had begged Adam to ask Mr. Brooks for help on the Miss Bloch story. She insisted that this was different from World Domination. She kept saying, "You're wrong; he'll help—you're his favorite." She said sometimes it was easier for a person like Mr. Brooks to stand up for someone else than for himself. She said maybe Mr. Brooks had personal reasons for not wanting to be the center of attention, but he might not mind helping on this one little point when it wasn't all about him.

Adam couldn't do it. He couldn't bear watching this teacher he thought he admired groveling out of another fight with Marris.

"No, Mr. Brooks," Adam answered. "Nothing's wrong, just really busy."

The teacher eyed him. "How's the November issue of the *Dash* coming along? I tell you, that October issue was so good, it will be a hard act for you to follow."

Adam nodded. Mr. Brooks didn't know the half of it. Adam was getting a pretty certain feeling that the November *Dash* would be their final act.

"Working on any interesting stories?" asked Mr. Brooks. "Or is that privileged information?"

Adam shrugged. "Just the usual."

Now Mr. Brooks nodded.

The older Adam got, the more he talked to adults, the more confused and disappointed he was. He felt like such a moron for thinking adults knew everything. One of the things he'd liked about Mr. Brooks was the man's ideas always seemed fresh. Now that Adam had come to know him a little behind the scenes, he realized Mr. Brooks could blather on just like the rest of them.

"Mr. Brooks," said Adam, "I'll try to have a better view of the world. I promise. Is there anything else? I've got to get to voluntary/mandatory."

Mr. Brooks raised his eyebrows. "Certainly wouldn't want to be late for that."

Adam smiled. "Yeah, we're probably practicing sharpening number-two pencils today." He picked up his backpack to leave.

"Um, Adam," said Mr. Brooks. "I don't quite know how to say this. When I was at Harvard a hundred years ago, they didn't teach journalism. It was considered a trade, like plumbing or bricklaying. So I don't really know the formal rules of the journalist. But this . . . I guess you'd call him a *source*—from the Latin, by the way, *surgere* . . . Well, this source-person told me that you kids might need some help for a story you're doing on Mrs. Marris."

Adam froze, too surprised to say a word. He didn't even remember to nod.

"I think the source-person's precise words were, 'They got the goods on that witch this time.' Well, what I'm trying to say," Mr. Brooks continued, "is that if I can be of assistance, I'd be delighted."

Had someone cut the wires between Adam's central nervous system and his neck? He was trying to nod, but his muscles weren't working.

"And this source-person," Mr. Brooks went on, "explained to me about not being in a position to be quoted by name. I think he said he was off the cuff. Well, what I want you to know is, you can use my name. It's all right. Of course, I can only help with what I know, and I don't know much, but if I understand the situation, you don't need much from me."

Suddenly Adam's synapses must have thawed or reconnected or done whatever synapses do to get back to business, because he was nodding at a ferocious clip, like one of those bobble-head dolls given out for prizes at the video arcade.

"You, of course, will have to explain the whole story to me," said Mr. Brooks. "I must be sure what I am telling you is placed in a fair context. . . . Adam, are you OK? . . . If you're not careful, you're going to nod your head right off your neck."

Was Adam OK? He had never been more OK. He was dying to ask Mr. Brooks why he'd decided to help them. Maybe Jennifer did have it right. But Adam caught himself. He didn't want to say anything that might spook Mr. Brooks.

This much Adam was sure of: A good reporter needs to know what questions NOT to ask.

It took a long time to lay out the whole story for Mr. Brooks. Adam loved telling it. He felt like he was in one of those extra-credit handouts Mr. Brooks had given them from a Plato dialogue. To Adam, Mr. Brooks sounded like Socrates: "Is it not true . . . ?" "Can we not assume . . . ?" "Do I understand you to say . . . ?" And Adam was the star pupil at the Academy.

It was after five when they finished. They decided that the story needed just one quote from Mr. Brooks. Adam had taken down a comment Mr. Brooks made, and then, together, they worked on getting it as clear and concise as possible. They agreed the finished sentence in the *Dash* would say:

> According to Prescott Brooks, a teacher at Harris, "When I asked about the work being done in her office, Mrs. Marris said it was all made possible with a gift from a woman who had recently died."

Adam kept thanking Mr. Brooks, but the teacher waved him off.

"Thank you," he said. "You know, I fear we've gone on so long, you've missed voluntary/mandatory."

"That's OK," said Adam. "I feel pretty confident about sharpening number-two pencils." He started to go, then turned back. "Mr. Brooks, I wanted to ask. A friend told me, there was a reporter who made a president resign?"

"Oh yes," said Mr. Brooks. "Two reporters. Bob Woodward and Carl Bernstein of the *Washington Post*. Their stories back in the 1970s on political corruption forced President Nixon from office."

Adam paused. "They didn't wind up in chains or die in poverty and neglect or anything like that, did they?"

"Oh no," said Mr. Brooks. "On the contrary. There was a movie about them—did quite well at the box office, as I remember."

Adam slapped the startled Mr. Brooks five and ran out the door, shouting, *"Ave atque vale!"*

"Animosus atque fortis appare!" Mr. Brooks called after him.

Several seconds passed and Adam's head appeared back in the door. "What was that?" Adam asked. "Don't think I know that one."

"Animosus atque fortis appare," Mr. Brooks repeated. "Be bold!"

The phone rang at the *Dash.* "Adam Canfield there?" asked the caller. It was a man.

"He's out on assignment," said Jennifer. "Can I help you?"

The man said he had some information about the basketball hoop crackdown that Mr. Canfield might find interesting.

Jennifer explained that she had worked on the story with Adam.

"Oh, you're the Jennifer byline," said the man. "Great job. Listen, are you guys planning a follow-up? Because I think I may have something for you."

The man explained that he was a zoning lawyer with a firm that had offices downtown, on top of the bank. He said he represented several people trying to stop Code Enforcement from tearing down the hoops.

"We went into court today to get a TRO," said the lawyer. "I think we have an excellent chance.

The judge seemed sympathetic. If we can get the TRO, I don't think they'll be able to get it lifted."

Jennifer's mind was racing. What was a *tiaroh*? It must be really heavy if they couldn't lift it. She tried thinking of legal stuff she'd heard her dad say at home. She remembered something about squishing subpoenas and vacationing in junctions, but lifting a *tiaroh*? Rang no bells. She hated sounding stupid to a grownup. Maybe he'd lose confidence and change his mind about helping. The only thing that kept popping into her head was beauty queens wearing *tiaras*. She considered bluffing her way through and trying to figure it out, but then decided to take a chance and admit her ignorance. Their minister always said ignorance is no shame if you're willing to learn your way out of it. "I'm sorry," Jennifer said. "I feel stupid, but what's a *tiaroh*?"

It worked like a charm. The lawyer told her there's nothing he respects more than reporters who know what they don't know. "It's the ones who know everything who do all the harm," he said. "Like that idiot Peter Friendly, on News 12. The man's a ticking time bomb."

The lawyer told Jennifer a TRO was a temporary restraining order. The lawyer said that if someone is

271

about to do something to you — like tear down your hoop — and you believe it is unfair, you can go to court and try to convince a judge that tearing down the hoop would cause serious harm. The judge has the power to issue a temporary restraining order — a TRO — to stop Code Enforcement from tearing down any hoops in Tremble until a full-blown trial can be held.

"I think we're going to win," said the lawyer. "I'll let you know. But that's not why I'm calling."

He told Jennifer that the hearing before the judge that morning was the most bizarre legal proceeding he had ever witnessed. "You met these Herbs, right?" said the lawyer. "Are those guys the whacko brothers?"

The lawyer said the Herbs had made all kinds of incredible statements and that Jennifer might want to use some of it in her next story. "I have a copy of the hearing I can send you," the lawyer continued. "I won't send the whole thing — it went on for three hours. I'll just e-mail a few pages of the transcript. Any questions, call me."

When Jennifer got home, she went right to her computer and opened the attachment from the lawyer.

It was part of his courtroom interview of Herb Black, and it must have been from the middle of the hearing—the first page the lawyer e-mailed was 108.

LAWYER: Now, Mr. Black, are basketball hoops ever actually mentioned in local law 200-52.7A?

HERB BLACK: Not per se.

L: Does that mean "no?"

HB: Yes.

L: Yes, it means no?

HB: That's right, yes, it means no.

L: So, if basketball hoops are not actually mentioned, it's a matter of interpretation when deciding what an accessory structure is?

HB: That's right—decided by experts based on years of rigorous Code Enforcement experience.

L: And those experts, would that be you and Herb Green?

HB: The very ones. Herb and Herb.

L: So, for example, would a lamppost out front of a house be considered an accessory structure? Should all the lampposts be torn down?

HB: Oh, come on. Lampposts are no accessory. They're essential. They provide light.

L: What about those little jockey statues that decorate the front drives of some of our large mansions here in Tremble?

HB: You mean the ones with black faces, big lips, and big white eyeballs?

L: That's right.

HB: Hmmm. You're asking if they're accessory structures. Hmmm. This is one of those trick lawyer questions, isn't it?

L: And how about flagpoles, Mr. Black? Do you consider them to be accessory structures? Should they be torn down?

HB: Hmmm. That would be something Herb and I would have to do further research to . . .

L: Mr. Black. Let me ask you this. Are you familiar with the plywood cow on Breckenridge, in the front yard of the big white house? It's sort of a landmark in the community.

HB: Of course. Herb and I must've passed it a hundred times while we were out red-tagging hoops.

L: And by any chance, did you hear someone had stolen the cow? And that it was returned?

HB: Oh sure. There was a nice story about it on Channel 12. Very fine piece of journalism, may I add. Had a happy ending, unlike most of the crap you see in the papers.

L: You were pleased to hear the cow was back, Mr. Black?

HB: Look, I know what you're trying to do. You're trying to show me and Herb are heartless zoning robots taking away the poor little children's basketball hoops. I know your schemey lawyer tricks. You're trying to make yourself out like you're some hero zoning lawyer—big Z on your chest—number one for the people. Well, I guarantee you, sir, a large heart beats beneath this chest, and the same goes for Herb Green sitting over there. You better believe, we Herbs, we were just as happy as the next guy when we heard the cow was back. Herb and I were jumping for joy; we were screaming, "Thank God the cow is back! Welcome back, cow!"

L: Mr. Black, you were cheering that someone was putting up an accessory structure in the front half of a housing lot? Shouldn't you have been out there red-tagging that cow? Shouldn't you have fined the owner five hundred dollars a day? After seven days, under local law 200-52.7A, wasn't it your duty to rip down that cow?

HB: Whoa, Mr. Smarty-Pants Lawyer. You think you have the Herbs painted into a corner? You think you're some hotshot making us look like hypocrites, right? Well, you're the hypocrite, Mr. Big-Z-on-Your-Chest. You know darned well that the zoning law can be twisted to mean anything you want it to!

chapter 18

Bring a Flashlight

The Tuesday evening before Thanksgiving was Eddie the Janitor Appreciation Night. It was a huge success. More than seven hundred parents, teachers, and friends crowded into the Harris auditorium. Perhaps most amazing, Eddie claimed to be surprised. For weeks the lower grades had secretly been practicing for the assembly. The second graders had prepared "When the Saints Go Marching In," but it wasn't until the big night that they stopped singing "the saints" and sang, "When Eddie James goes marching in . . ." The first graders were ready with "Thank Heavens for Eddie James," but it was the kindergarteners who stole the show, belting out those classic Paul McCartney lyrics, "Eddie, we're amazed at the way we love you all the time; Eddie, we're amazed at the way we really love you. . . ." There were "Thank You, Eddie" balloons and an eighty-stanza poem written by Marsha Tiffany Glickman, the editor of *Sketches*, the Harris literary magazine, entitled "Ode to Eddie James."

The *Dash* staff had blown up the front-page photo of Eddie and the two mourning doves into a five-foot poster along with a laminated copy of Phoebe's article.

The Tremble Janitors' Association gave him an engraved gold key holder that he could attach to his belt, and the PTA had a potted plant for him with one thousand dollars in cash taped to the branches.

They were tricky about getting Eddie onstage. The PTA tri-presidents started to welcome everybody but then pretended the microphone wasn't working. Eddie was standing at the rear of the auditorium. At the first hint of trouble, he rushed up to help. As he would later tell Phoebe for her story in the *Dash*, "I saw some black folks onstage, and coming up the aisle, I realized they was my family."

Eddie was not exactly the perfect honoree. He

278

had trouble standing in one place and being praised. When the microphone squealed during a speech enumerating his virtues, Eddie ran behind the curtain and adjusted the treble. During refreshments, he insisted on manning the coffee table. Each time they tried to get him to sit with his family, he said, "You know I'm not much at sitting; I'm a service person."

The most asked question was, "Were you really surprised?" And each time Eddie answered, "Totally," although people couldn't be sure since Eddie *was* a service person and pleasing others was his primary service.

So many people made speeches, the celebration lasted over two hours.

There was just one sour note. Miss Esther had called the tri-presidents that afternoon to say that Mrs. Marris was feeling sick to her stomach and would not be attending.

Mrs. Marris must have had a twenty-four-hour flu — or maybe even a shorter twelve-hour economy version — because when they arrived at school next morning, there she was, standing in the hallway by the main office, a smile plastered in place, saying good morning to everybody and hurrying them along to home base.

There was excitement in the air; this was the last day of school before the long Thanksgiving weekend.

Adam spied Marris and put his head down, trying to blend into the crowd and flow on by, but it didn't work.

"Adam Canfield," she called out. Was that menace in her voice or was Adam imagining it? "Adam," she repeated. "Am I going to see my copy of the *Dash* this morning?"

Adam figured it was good they were in a public place, so Marris probably would not shoot him or bludgeon him to death with so many witnesses around.

"It's nearly done," he lied. "You'll have it first thing Monday."

"I better," she said. "November's almost gone." The crowd of kids was thinning out. Fewer witnesses. "I know it's going to have that story on Miss Bloch, am I right?" She was smiling, but her eyes reminded Adam of an owl he had seen on a Discovery Channel special, right before it swooped down, grabbed a mouse by the tail, and flew off for supper. Adam identified with that mouse, its pitiful butt shaking in terror high above the forest floor. At this moment, Adam needed all his powers of concentration to keep from busting out in the shakes himself.

"Oh yes," he said. "It will have the Miss Bloch story. That will definitely be in there, Mrs. Marris. If there's one thing that's absolutely certain, it's the Miss Bloch story for page 1."

Marris leaned toward him, smiling hard, and in a voice that only he could hear, whispered, "It damn well better be."

That long weekend was a blur of work for Adam, Jennifer, and most of the *Dash* staff. It wasn't just the Miss Bloch story. Phoebe was writing up Eddie Appreciation Night. Sammy and the Spotlight Team were finishing their articles on the cafeteria food.

Jennifer was handling the follow-up to the hoop story, and there were plenty of fresh developments on that front. On Wednesday afternoon Jennifer got another e-mail from the zoning lawyer. The judge had granted the restraining order. The county was prohibited from tearing down "all basketball structures red-tagged in the last thirty days under local law 200-52.7A."

The hoops were saved! At least for the time being. The zoning lawyer said he had more news, but it was too much for an e-mail, and asked that Jennifer call him. Because of the holiday, he even gave her his home number.

She reached him that night. His daughter answered. When the little girl heard it was the *Dash*, she got excited.

"Is this about the basketball hoop stowy?" she said. "Have we got gweat news! The little childwen have been saved! Victowy is at hand! Hold on, I'll get Daddy."

The lawyer explained that the county zoning board could still appeal the judge's ruling, but he didn't think that would happen, based on a conversation he had with the Tremble County attorney. It was the county attorney who represented the Herbs and the zoning board. It was the county attorney who was supposed to fight for Tremble's right to tear down the hoops. But halfway through the hearing, it was the county attorney who started sinking lower and lower in his chair. "By the time the hearing was over," the zoning lawyer told Jennifer, "you could barely see the county attorney's head. Afterward, I made a wisecrack about what great witnesses the

Herbs were. And the county attorney says, 'If you added the Herbs together, their combined IQ would not reach three digits.'"

There was more. At the hearing, the people who organized the petition drive presented the judge all the signatures they'd collected. "Thousands of names," said the zoning lawyer. "I stopped counting at three thousand. I thought the county attorney would be furious, but he just winked at me and whispered, 'Thank God for democracy.'"

"The way I figure it," the zoning lawyer said, "thousands of signatures represent thousands of votes. If there's one thing the top politicians in Tremble stand for, if there's just one principle they hold dearer than all others, it is getting themselves reelected. I'm pretty sure we've heard the last of the basketball hoop crackdown."

Jennifer was thrilled, but overwhelmed by all the work still to do. After hanging up, she e-mailed Adam a brief summary, then collapsed into bed, exhausted.

Thanksgiving morning Adam usually went with his father and Danny to the Turkey Classic, the annual football matchup between Tremble High and North Tremble High, but this year he skipped the game to work on the Miss Bloch story. He had to finish a rough draft so he and Jennifer could go over it together. Even more important, they needed to figure out how to deal with Marris on Monday morning. It was a cardinal rule of journalism, they knew, that you had to get a comment—or at least try to—from the person you were writing about.

But what if that person also had the power to decide what did or did not go into the newspaper? The moment they asked Marris about the gold plumbing, it was obvious to Adam that she would go ballistic and order them to kill the story.

Adam felt maybe they didn't need a comment from Marris. After all, she had already given them her version of the Miss Bloch story way back in September. That might be enough.

Writing the first draft was not too bad. Adam found when he had done all the reporting for an article, the writing went quickly. The hard stories were the ones full of reporting holes that you tried to hide with fancy writing.

Friday and Saturday the three typists e-mailed in stories. This time Adam and Jennifer agreed about the front page. For the top left of page 1 they chose the basketball piece. Jennifer wrote the headline: "Hoops Saved!" Underneath it, the subhead read: "Judge Halts Zoning Crackdown."

Beneath that story, stripped across the middle of the page, was the Spotlight Team report: "Cafeteria Food = Low Grade." To accompany that piece and the two other Spotlight articles running inside, a girl in art workshop had designed a cartoon logo of a spotlight shining on a green hot dog.

On the bottom of the page was Phoebe's story on Eddie.

That left only the Miss Bloch story, which was to go at the top right of page 1.

Several times the coeditors argued over whether they needed to give Marris a second chance to explain herself. Jennifer said yes. She reminded Adam about a PBS *Frontline* documentary she'd watched on a reporter who had not given the subject a fair chance to reply and how it had turned into a multizillion-dollar lawsuit.

Truth was, neither of them knew what to do. They needed help from a grownup but didn't want to ask their parents. Adam was afraid his mom and dad either wouldn't believe that Marris was a crook or would want him to kill the story because Adam would get into too much trouble. Jennifer's parents were so involved in the PTA, and the PTA seemed to do whatever Marris wanted. Would a PTA person ever believe Marris stole seventy-five thousand dollars? Jennifer knew PTA members did lots of good, but when it came to Marris, they seemed to be the number-one principal-kiss-up organization.

Jennifer had been amazed when her mom actually had believed that Marris was too sick to attend Eddie's party.

Finally, Adam said, "Danny. We could go see Danny."

Jennifer liked that. Danny did seem like one of those rare adults who still had some kid in him. Besides, it would be another chance to visit all those adorable dogs and cats. Jennifer was really in the mood to have some cute animal take one look at her and instantly fall in love.

They agreed to meet at the shelter after Jennifer got back from church.

By Saturday night they had the whole paper ready, except the lead story. They left that space blank.

In the car on the way home from Adam's house, Jennifer sat in the dark, not saying a word. Her mother asked if everything was all right. "Whatchya thinking about, sweetie?" her mother said.

"Nothing," said Jennifer, but it wasn't true. At church on Sunday their minister always reserved time for a personal prayer. Jennifer wondered if it would be a misuse of the power of prayer to ask God for help on the Marris story.

When Jennifer pulled up to the animal shelter on her bike, Adam was already there.

Adam, she thought, getting places early. This Marris story was making them crazy. They hurried up the front steps and asked the receptionist to call Danny.

After a few minutes, the phone at the desk rang. The woman motioned for Adam and, stretching the cord, handed him the receiver.

"Hey, Adam," Danny said. "Look, I'm sorry. It's going to be awhile. I'm in the operating room, assisting our surgeon. We've got a six-year-old with heart failure. Doc's pumping him full of Isopurel, gave him a shot of epinephrine to jolt the heart, but the EKG looks bleak. I'll be out as soon as I can."

It was nearly a half-hour before Danny appeared.

Adam took one look and knew the news was bad. "Lost him," said Danny. "Sweetheart of a dog, too. Lovely disposition. A big-hearted Lab. Too big, as a matter of fact. Enlarged. Leaky valve. Cardiac arrest, 12:58 P.M. I had to finish filling out the certificate."

They followed Danny through the door into the high-ceilinged room full of chainlink cages. But this time, instead of rushing on to the adoption arena, Danny paused and greeted the animals. Then he walked to a bench in a corner and slumped down. Adam and Jennifer joined him.

"I hate it when we lose one," he said. "Doesn't happen often, but when it does, I just can't go marching back out to the arena and fire off a bunch of brilliant matches like everything's normal. I need to collect myself, sit here among the dogs and cats. Reminds me why we're here."

"We need your help," said Adam.

"I doubt I can be much use. My specialty's animals," said Danny. "People never cease to confuse me."

"Remember last time we came, to ask about Miss Bloch?" said Adam. "Well, we solved the mystery."

"We solved lots of mysteries," said Jennifer, and

right there, amid the barking and meowing, they told Danny the long, sordid story of Marris's scheme.

Danny listened without interrupting. When they'd finished, his reaction stunned them. "Poor Ruth Ellen," said Danny.

"Poor Ruth Ellen!" Adam repeated. "Poor Ruth Ellen! What about poor us? She stole the children's money, and she's probably going to kill us for telling the truth about it. You don't think it's true?"

"Oh, I didn't say that," Danny said. "It rings one hundred percent true to me. Sounds exactly like the Ruth Ellen Marris I knew."

"Then what?" said Adam. "I thought you told us even in third grade she was a liar and weasel."

"And a snitch and a suck-up and a phony and a bragger and an all-around nasty person," said Danny. "I hated her."

"Then what?" said Adam.

"I don't know," said Danny. "Maybe it's because the dog died, but it just seems so sad sometimes that people can't help being what they are. Ruth Ellen Marris didn't come from one of the rich Tremble families, but she sure wanted to. Some kids, they don't notice those differences, and some do but keep

289

it to themselves until they're grown. But Ruth Ellen, even as a girl, I remember her playing up to the rich la-la girls and bragging about how well-to-do her family was. Such sad, sad lies. You know how kids can be so mean to a girl like that, especially when she is so naked about wanting to be popular? It's a hard thing to watch, naked ambition. It sears the eyeballs. And Ruth Ellen was the nakedest."

Adam was using all his powers to envision Mrs. Marris with lots and lots of clothes on. "You think we shouldn't do the story?" Adam asked.

"Oh no," said Danny. "I didn't say that. You have to do the story. I'd bet a million dollars this isn't the first time she's taken money. Just because it's sad or understandable doesn't excuse it. I guarantee there are five hundred prisoners at the county jail, with five hundred sob stories every bit as sad as *Billboard* magazine's five hundred top country-and-western hits. You must do the story."

They asked Danny if he thought they needed to go back to Marris for her side of things. Adam explained that he and Jennifer disagreed.

"I'm with the True Gladiator on this one," said Danny. "This is very serious business, calling a principal a thief. Can't take any shortcuts."

Jennifer asked what they should do when Marris told them they couldn't print the story.

"Don't print it," said Danny. "You certainly can't disobey your principal."

Adam and Jennifer stared at him.

"Oh, come on," said Danny. "Think. I've got a True Gladiator and a four-pluser, and you're looking at me like I'm speaking Croatian. I'll tell you what. You go home right now and I'll e-mail you the solution."

"E-mail the solution?" asked Adam.

"E-mail the solution!" shouted Jennifer. She grabbed Adam's hands and they twirled each other around in an impromptu e-mail-the-solution dance, serenaded by hundreds of excited dogs and cats.

They had a backup plan, finally. "If I were you," said Danny. "I'd get together all the kids from the *Dash* and have them create a list of every e-mail address they know, adults especially. Have them get into their parents' mailboxes and get any names they can. You want this reaching as many important people as possible. Make calls, get e-mail addresses for school board members, politicians, business-people, the police, the district attorney's office."

"We've got to get the whole staff together," said Jennifer.

"It's got to be tonight," said Adam. "We're just about out of time. We'll have to let everyone know this afternoon, as soon as we get home."

"We can meet at my house," said Jennifer.

Adam shook his head. "I don't think we can afford to tell parents," he said. "They might try to stop us."

"Maybe we could get into the *Dash* office," said Jennifer. "Phoebe could call Eddie. He'd have the key."

"No way," said Adam. "If just one adult driving by saw the light, we'd be found out and Eddie would get fired."

Danny said they could use his apartment, but he lived too far away. They'd need rides, and that would involve parents, too.

Suddenly Adam shouted, "I know where no one will ever find us. All we'll need is flashlights."

chapter 19

A Secret Meeting

They began arriving at the boathouse at Long Bluff a little before 7:30. When Adam rode up, he could make out a half-dozen bikes already there, parked in the dark along the boardwalk fence. It was cold — the wind was whipping off the river, bending trees, and making branches creak. Kids were huddled by the front door, bouncing up and down for warmth, waiting for Adam to let them in.

Getting a key had been no problem. Adam's dad was on the civic association board, and Jennifer's mom was one of the garden club women who planted the boathouse flower boxes. Adam had simply sneaked his father's key off the hook in the kitchen.

He hid his bike in the bluff grass in case anyone came along the path at that hour, and passed the word that they should all do the same. It was a moonless night. He could see the house lights on the bank on the far side of the river; he could see the flashing green light of a buoy bobbing on the river. But he had trouble seeing anything right around him. As he moved across the bluff toward the boathouse, he stumbled frequently, scratching his hand on a thornbush. Little drops of blood beaded on his palm.

The lock was so rusted, he kept jiggling the key but it wouldn't catch. "Come on, come on," he kept urging, and finally there was a click. It was pitch-black inside. The windows were boarded up, the electricity was switched off, and there was no heat. They stationed a boy by the door to guide latecomers to the meeting.

Holding their flashlights, they walked down the hallway toward the big room overlooking the river. They moved in one large group, pressing together for reassurance. When one slipped, several of them bumped, startling everyone. The floorboards creaked with every step, and the wind whooshed through the gaps in the walls. Below they could hear the water lapping and crashing against the boathouse pillars. Once in a while a big swell would dash against the rocks on the shore's edge, and then as it withdrew, there'd be a loud sucking noise that sounded like some awful river beast howling in pain.

The hallway walls were lined with black-and-white photos of past boathouse commodores. Danny had once joked to Adam that a civic association commodore was one rank below an army private, but Adam wasn't laughing tonight. In every photo the commodores wore the same white sailing caps with anchors on the brims and navy blue coats with bunting on the shoulders. Under each portrait was the year they had been commodore. A lot were from the 1930s and 1940s. Staring out of the dark in the wobbly glow of flashlights, all of them smiling and yet so long-ago dead—it gave Adam the creeps.

The door to the big room was slightly ajar, and when Adam opened it all the way, something living tumbled down on them.

Whatever it was fell right past Adam's face, brushing his coat. More kept falling. One bounced off a girl's head. "I'm being attacked," she shrieked. "Claws!"

They were screaming now, Adam's heart was in

his throat, and one of the typists yelled, "I want my mommy!"

But then the calmest, most matter-of-fact voice Adam had ever heard said, "Relax. Just a bunch of mice. Must have been eight or ten of them piled together for warmth on top of the door ledge. Nice safe place for a mouse. We startled them. Nothing to fear, folks."

Adam's jaw dropped. Phoebe! She went on to explain that one of her older brothers had trained mice to run through a maze for a science project, and she had learned to pick them up, discovering the truth about mice—they were fraidy cats.

"Now rats," continued Phoebe, "that's another matter. If anyone sees a rat tonight, I would immediately—"

"Phoebe, thanks for your help," said Adam. "You were a calm voice in the storm. We've got to get down to business now. We don't have much time. If we're gone too long, our parents will know something's up."

"Adam," said Phoebe, "you and Jennifer are our fearless leaders. We are with you one hundred percent. If you order us to jump, we will say, 'How high, sir?' If you tell us to 'Charge!' we'll hand over our parents' credit cards. If you say, 'Duck!' we'll quack. The only thing I thought might be worth mentioning, sir—when I heard this afternoon that this was going to be the secret meeting place, I looked up *river rats* and *rat bites*—they can be quite serious, sir. If anyone—"

"PHOEBE!" yelled Adam. "STOP TALKING!"

"I can't," said Phoebe. "My mother says it's a nervous reaction. When I get scared, I just talk and talk and—"

"Front-Page," said Jennifer in a soothing voice, "come over here beside me. Come on." The older girl put her arm around the younger girl, who immediately stopped babbling. It was like Jennifer had pulled out Phoebe's plug. Adam could not believe how Jennifer figured out this kind of stuff.

They moved a bunch of the canvas chairs and wicker sofas into a circle. It was amazing. The entire *Dash* staff—all twenty-three—had made it. They were a hardy bunch, all right. Jennifer and Adam explained the Marris story as quickly as they could. They didn't give all the details—just enough so everyone would understand why Marris would want to kill them and why they might not be able to print the *Dash* the usual way.

297

"This will all come out in the next few days," said Jennifer. "If we do this right, everybody in Tremble will know. But until it happens, this has to be top secret. If Marris finds out, who knows what she'd do to us."

"Top secret," repeated Phoebe, "Tippity-top secret. The tippity-toppest. Very tippity . . ." Jennifer put her arm around her, rubbed her back a little, and Phoebe stopped.

Adam explained that they each had to put together a list of as many e-mail addresses of adults as they could. He assigned several to make calls Monday and get addresses for crucial grownups like school board members and elected officials.

A girl on the Spotlight Team suggested they could also get the story out by posting it at a website.

"There's no time," someone said.

"Yes, there is. That's a great idea," said Jennifer. "We don't have to make a special *Dash* web page with all the bells and whistles. We can just take one of those ready-made web page forms that kids use to make sites for boyfriends and girlfriends."

It was a terrific idea, but Adam didn't feel terrific. How did Jennifer know about those lovey-dovey sites? Did she have some boyfriend she was making websites for? He had been so sure Jennifer wasn't like that. Had she turned into that kind of girl when he wasn't paying attention? It was frustrating; there was so much to keep track of. A heavy feeling filled his chest.

"I've never done it myself," Jennifer continued, glancing toward Adam, who suddenly was beaming like a thousand flashlights. "It would be great if a typist . . ."

"I'll do it," said the girl who just minutes before had been calling for her mommy. That's how things were going—the longer the meeting went on, the braver they felt.

Of course, there would be nothing for the *Dash* staff to e-mail to all those important grownups and nothing to post at a romance website until Adam finished writing the story. And Adam couldn't finish until he and Jennifer interviewed Marris on Monday morning. He began calculating. Assuming they survived the interview—assuming Marris didn't have them locked up in the county juvenile detention hall—Adam still had to work her comments into the story. Then he would have to type the article into the computer himself, and he was a painfully slow keyboarder. Then he would have to e-mail Jennifer the final draft so she could look it over, make changes, and e-mail it back to him.

It was going to be Monday night, maybe midnight, maybe later, by the time he was done and ready to forward the Marris story to everyone.

"OK, listen up," he said. "Obviously if Marris has a reasonable explanation for what she did with the seventy-five thousand dollars, we'll just write up a regular article and send an e-mail telling you to forget it. But if this goes like we think, by the time Jennifer and I finish writing and editing, it will be really late. And that's going to be a problem."

Everyone started talking at once. Several said they'd love to stay up all Monday night, and people began announcing their record for the latest they'd been awake at sleepovers.

"We think it would be a big mistake to do anything that would give your parents the idea that something's up," said Jennifer. "Even my mom—I love her a ton, but she's in the PTA and they're so tight with Marris. We don't want to give Marris a clue how we're getting this story out until it's too late."

Some said they had alarm clocks in their rooms or on their watches that they could set, and others suggested forwarding the story in the morning before they went to school, but Adam thought that was too risky. "I don't know about you," he said, "but when I set my alarm clock—the one who wakes up is my father.

"I'm going to tell you something I've never told anyone before," Adam continued. "It's my foolproof method for waking myself up in the middle of the night. I use it in the winter when it's supposed to snow and I want to get up early to see if it really did, so I'll know if we're going to have a snow day."

He paused. He was a little embarrassed to say it in front of girls and stalled, trying to think of the right words. When he finally told everybody, his voice was so soft, they had to lean forward and strain to hear. A little mouse in the corner of that boathouse trying to listen in would have missed it.

And then suddenly, as they all understood what it was, they laughed, they howled, they thought it hilarious, outrageous, brilliant in its simplicity. They were totally in love with, totally sold on Adam Canfield's 100 percent guaranteed, foolproof middle-of-the-night wake-up system. They crushed in around him, they were so excited, and slapped him high-fives, pushed him affectionately, punched him in the shoulder. Sammy gave him a bear hug and lifted him off the ground.

When he came back down to earth, Adam said, "The only thing is, after you go, don't flush the toilet. You don't want to wake anybody."

chapter 20

Expulsion

His dad had to come in three times to wake him on Monday morning. After Adam's head cleared, he lay there savoring the boathouse meeting. It was their finest hour. He'd felt so sure of himself as they'd all jumped on their bikes and raced home through the dark.

Then everything began pressing down on him. He was seized by panic. Marris! He sat straight up in bed. Marris! They had the meeting today. It always amazed him how you could go to bed feeling like a million bucks and wake up needing change for a nickel. How would they pull it off? When they turned up in her office without the *Dash*, she was going to— Adam shut his mind down and jumped out of bed. He did not want to follow that thought through to its logical conclusion.

His dad had to take an early train and had left out a glass of milk along with several cereal snack boxes for him. Adam did not have the energy to choose one. He'd never been much of a breakfast eater, although most days he would at least pick the marshmallow bits out of the Lucky Charms. This morning, the thought of food made him sick. Right before he was to walk out the door to catch the bus, he dropped his backpack and baritone and raced to the bathroom, where he retched and heaved. His stomach was empty, nothing came up, but he lay flat on the bathroom floor, staring at the ceiling, convinced he was too sick to go to school.

This hadn't happened to him since he was a four-year-old, terrified of starting kindergarten. He tried to remind himself that he was Adam Canfield of the *Dash*, but sprawled on the bathroom floor, he felt so small, so unimportant, an impostor in his own skin.

* * *

As he climbed off the bus, he spotted Jennifer waiting by the flagpole. She gave him a big smile. "Ready?" she said. "You did great last night."

"No," he said weakly. "You did."

She looked him over. "You OK?" she asked. "No offense, but you look really white."

"I'm like a total wreck," he said. He told her about getting sick. He said he wasn't sure if he could go through with the Marris meeting. He suggested they put it off a day.

"Listen," Jennifer said. "You know how my father's always making me read biographies of famous black people?" And then she told him about a book she'd just done a report on, about Bill Russell, a great basketball player for the Boston Celtics from long ago. Before all the big games, the book said, Russell would be in the locker room throwing up from nerves. "And then he'd go out and dominate," Jennifer continued. "He won more NBA championships than Jordan, Shaq, and Magic."

"If we were just playing for the NBA championship, I'd be fine," said Adam.

Together, they walked into school. Once again Marris was standing by her office welcoming everyone back from Thanksgiving, the signature smile shining bright. "Holiday's over, boys and girls," she kept saying. "Let's zip those lips. I hope you all have your thinking caps on. Lots of work between now and Christmas. We're going to be busy, busy, so tighten those thinking caps for liftoff."

Before Marris spotted them, Jennifer called out, "Mrs. Marris! Hi, over here. Yoo-hoo! Can we talk to you?" Jennifer waved.

Adam could not believe this. He was hoping that somehow they could just slip by and wait to be called down to the office. Maybe Marris would have a heart attack or die of cancer during second period. What was Jennifer yoo-hooing about? He'd never heard Jennifer yoo-hoo before.

Yoo-hoo, Adam thought to himself, we're ready to face the firing squad now, Mrs. Marris. Yoo-hoo, drop the guillotine blade now, Mrs. Marris. Yoo-hoo, it's a convenient time for the lethal injection.

"When do you want to see us about the *Dash*?" Jennifer asked coolly.

Mrs. Marris paused, then said, "Why don't we do it right now? Let's get it over with."

They followed her out of the noisy corridor and into the outer office. Adam had expected more time to prepare. He wasn't ready. He'd been counting on having several periods to psyche himself up.

"How about if you just give me the *Dash* proof and wait here," said Mrs. Marris. "I'll take it to my office, do a quick read, then call you down for my edits. It'll go faster that way."

"We wanted to talk to you about that," said Jennifer. "The November issue's not quite done."

Marris froze. She glared. Her mouth opened like she wanted to bite something; Adam had never noticed how sharp her eyeteeth looked.

"Let me explain," said Jennifer, and she started talking about how hard they'd worked over Thanksgiving break.

Adam knew he should say something. Poor Jennifer was doing all the talking. What was wrong with him? Maybe he'd come down with lockjaw. He'd seen a science special about how this pernicious disease was becoming a real problem in Africa. It was his parents' fault; they'd forgotten to get him his tetanus booster. He was letting everyone down. He had to say something.

"Was your Thanksgiving joyous, Mrs. Marris?" he blurted out. Jennifer and Marris both turned and stared at him. Why did he say that? Maybe he had early onset Alzheimer's. Doctors were finding it in people as young as their forties; scientists just didn't realize yet how incredibly early this devastating disease could strike. "We've been busy, busy," Adam said. "The entire Thanksgiving break we kept our thinking caps on."

"Cut that ridiculous babble," said Marris. "What's going on now?"

"We just had one story where we had a few questions for you," said Jennifer.

"One story," repeated Marris.

"The Miss Bloch story," said Jennifer.

"The Miss Bloch story again!" shouted Mrs. Marris. "The Miss Bloch story. What is it about that story that seems to be causing you such problems? It's been two months. I could have given it to a couple of linemen on the football team, and they'd have been done in two hours. What is wrong with you?"

Adam tried not to look her in the eye. He was thinking of that poor little Discovery Channel mouse being carried off by the owl, butt twitching. He was feeling pretty twitchy himself. What if he cried? All the good he had done until now would be ruined. He glanced around the room, anything not to meet

Marris's evil eye, and as he did, he caught a glimpse of Mrs. Rose's head.

He was shocked.

It was plain as day. He could see it on her face, in her eyes, around her mouth and forehead—an unmistakable look of sympathy. Even she knew what Marris was; in that instant Adam was sure of it. When he tried to catch Mrs. Rose's eye, she shuddered, her face flushed, and immediately she resumed her stone front. But that was all Adam needed. He had spotted weakness right in the palace's inner circle. He remembered Mr. Brooks's lesson: Even the mighty Caesar was vulnerable from those closest at hand. Brutus knew what a monster Caesar had become, and the permed head knew it about Marris. Adam could feel the energy surging back into his limbs. He was ready to play for the NBA title.

"Mrs. Marris," he said, "could we sit with you for a few minutes? We just have a couple of questions about the terms of Miss Bloch's gift."

She looked shocked, took a step toward them, seemed ready to attack, then pivoted and hurried off toward her office. There was a pause. No one knew what to do until Mrs. Rose's head motioned for them to sit.

In the next several minutes, the permed head rushed back and forth so many times, it wore Adam out watching. At one point Eddie hurried in, eyes straight ahead like he'd never met them, and disappeared down the Bunker stairs. He was gone a good fifteen or twenty minutes.

After he reemerged and left, the permed head rushed off, rushed back, and said, "She's ready."

Given all the activity, they had expected the Bunker would look different. Adam was thinking maybe Marris would have a torture rack set up. The reporters eyeballed the bathroom area in the rear for signs of a commotion, but the door was shut. Nothing seemed out of place.

They took seats, waiting for her to say something. Marris glared. The longer her silence lasted, the more frightening it grew. Adam was determined not to be cowed. He felt like they'd gained an advantage and he was not about to give it up. They had planned that Jennifer would ask the first questions while they slowly worked their way up to the most sensitive stuff, but now the dragon's underbelly was exposed. It was time to thrust the sword. Adam pounced.

"When you described the Miss Bloch gift to us in September, you said it could go to quote-unquote 'general improvements,'" Adam began. "But according to interviews we've done and a copy of Miss Bloch's will we've obtained, isn't it true that the money was supposed to be used for deserving—"

"Ohhhhhh," interrupted Mrs. Marris. "'According to interviews . . .' is it? Documents you've 'obtained . . .' is it? My busy little bees. You have been buzzing around, haven't you? BUZZ! BUZZ! BUZZ! YOU IDIOTS! BUZZ! BUZZ! BUZZ! YOU FOOLS! BUZZ! BUZZ! BUZZ! YOU NAIVE, SPOILED BRATS! You think you're so smart. A four-pluser and a True Gladiator. You think you were born with magic powers to protect you from all harm. Real children of privilege, aren't you? Suburban superheroes! You don't have a clue what life is about.

"Let me just fill you in, you seekers of truth. 'Isn't it true . . ?' you say. Truth. Ha! There's the Little Truth and there's the Big Truth. The Little Truth— that's the world where reporters dwell. This little true fact and this little true fact and this little true fact, and you pile them all together and you think you have a story. Well, I'm sorry to say, all those nice little true facts don't add up to the truth. You wouldn't be

311

interested in the Big Truth, would you? There's no room for the Big Truth in newspapers is there?

"The Big Truth is that principals work a million hours in the most primitive conditions and don't get paid a fraction of what they're worth. You weren't planning to put that in your article, were you? Who cares about principals—they're just public employees. Who cares about principals—they're mostly women; we can pay them less. Who cares—they're not doing anything important like manufacturing electric toothbrushes or managing stock portfolios for zillionaires. All they're doing is educating our youth. No big deal. Just the nation's entire future. No one thinks about all the extra hours the principal puts in with no extra pay, all those night meetings, all that paperwork that gets done at home. All the time spent teaching yet another idiot PTA president how to run a bake sale or breaking in a newly elected school board star so the fool knows where to stand at the Say No assembly. You're so worried about Miss Bloch's will. You're so worried about how the money was spent. You think a principal ever gets enough money for what she does? Truth! It's truth you're after? You don't have a clue what truth is, you . . . you . . . you . . . reporters!"

She took a key from her pocket, unlocked her middle drawer, pulled out two sheets of paper, and circled around her enormous desk to Adam and Jennifer. She stood over them now, glaring down. "You are not to print a word of that 'according to interviews' stuff or documents 'obtained' nonsense in that newspaper. You know darned well what I want that Miss Bloch story to say. Do you understand me? Do you know what these are?" She thrust the two sheets of paper in their faces. "Read them!" she screamed.

They were expulsion notices. Adam's and Jennifer's names had already been filled out at the top.

"Read the boxes I've checked," she said. "I'm not making this stuff up. It's there in black and white."

She had checked the box marked: *Insubordination — repeated refusal to follow orders from school district officials.*

She had checked the box marked: *Destruction or misuse of school property.* Beside this she had written: *Used school property — the* Dash — *for personal gain, to save their own basketball hoops from being torn down by county officials.*

For Adam, she had also checked: *Truancy—repeatedly skipped class for state competency test preparation.*

"Mark my words," Mrs. Marris said. "If you try, just try, to put one word of your big-shot Miss Bloch investigation in that paper, you will be expelled. These forms will immediately be whisked over to the superintendent's office. It will all go on your permanent record. And I want to remind you, they don't call it 'permanent' for nothing. We're talking totally permanent—we're talking about something that's going to follow you to the far corners of the earth. A thousand years from now when archaeologists dig up your pathetic remains, it will still be there, telling your ancestors what vermin you were.

"You can't imagine how impressed some fancy Ivy League college admissions office will be to see that you were expelled, Mr. Four-Plus and you, too, faithful sidekick Wonder Woman. Don't go thinking it will make a difference if your families hire some fancy-pants lawyer to get you off. That would take years of hearings and appeals; even if you beat it eventually, people will assume you're just rich kids who got off on a technicality.

"And the worst part of it for you—all this will be for nothing. Even if you do try to print it, you think I'd ever allow that paper to be handed out in home base? Fools!" Mrs. Marris grabbed the expulsion forms out of their hands, walked back around her desk, and made a big thing of sticking them in her middle drawer, locking it, and putting away the key. "It's your future, your choice," she said.

She came back around, stood behind them, then grabbed their collars, yanked them up, and pushed them toward the stairs. "Get out," she yelled as they stumbled forward. "I want you in here first thing tomorrow morning with the *Dash* proof. And it better not be full of those vicious lies."

Even if Adam and Jennifer had wanted to back down, they realized they couldn't. All day long, they ran into kids from the *Dash* wanting to know if the two of them had done the interview with Marris yet and how it had gone. Usually, when Adam was trying to track down some *Dash* reporter for an overdue story, he could go days without seeing the kid at school. Today it seemed like he bumped into every last staff member. "We on for tonight, sir?" Phoebe had whispered as she rushed past on her way to a class. And the big wink she'd given him along with the military salute had pierced his heart.

They couldn't let these people down now.

Adam realized that this must be how history got made. In a moment of bold dementia, you made a speech about how you were going to undertake this amazing plan if such-and-such happened. And then, when it happened, you had to go through with it, even though you realized too late that there were going to be lots of battlefield casualties.

The odd thing was, neither Adam nor Jennifer was as scared by the Marris meeting as they probably should have been. For Adam, the turning point had come when Marris started foaming about their permanent records. In his experience, teachers who threatened you with your permanent record were one step away from a nervous breakdown.

Maybe they had Marris on the run.

Maybe they didn't. As Jennifer once said, who knew with Marris?

At this point Adam just wanted it to be over. If he was expelled, he planned to sleep for a week.

Jennifer arranged with the print shop to have proofs made first thing Tuesday morning.

It was past midnight by the time the coeditors had e-mailed the final version of the lead story back and forth and felt they had it right.

By then the *Dash* members were snugly asleep in their beds. But before turning out the lights, they all had used the heralded Adam Canfield middle-of-the-night wake-up system. When it was time to brush their teeth for bed, they'd gone into the bathroom with a large drinking cup and closed the door.

They drank six tall glasses of water.

Then they went to sleep.

The littlest among them woke first. They had the smallest bladders and were up by 2 A.M., racing to the bathroom to take the most urgent, most enormous pee they could ever remember. The bigger ones with bigger bladders made it until 3 A.M. Then, per Adam's instructions, without flushing the toilet or turning on lights, they crept to their computers.

Computer screens glowing in the dark give off a pale blue light, but they were prepared for that, too.

They took a sheet from their beds and draped it over their terminals and their heads, creating a tent to hide the screen's glow.

Safe from view, they signed on. The story was there. Most didn't bother reading it right then; they wanted to be done with this treachery as quickly as possible. Still, they couldn't help noticing that Adam and Jennifer had included a little box with the article that said, "The following staff members also contributed to this story," and then named every *Dash* member.

They *were* contributing. They had already typed all the addresses for forwarding the story beside the carbon copy function in the header marked *cc.* They positioned the mouse at *send*, pressed *enter*, and in an instant the story was on the way, forwarded all over Tremble to hundreds and hundreds of important adults who would find it when they next opened their e-mail.

The typist contributed, too, posting the *Dash* investigation on a do-it-yourself romance website.

Within minutes, they emerged from their secret hideouts and were safe in bed.

Not one was caught.

The only thing the moms and dads noticed when

they woke Tuesday morning was toilets that needed flushing. But that was business as usual and aroused absolutely no suspicion.

Adam and Jennifer went straight to Mrs. Marris's office. Not even Adam wanted to put this off. They walked in, and immediately Mrs. Rose's head said, "She's waiting for you."

Marris was sitting behind her desk. Her face was expressionless. Adam handed her the *Dash* proof.

It was impossible to miss. On the top right half of the front page where the Miss Bloch story was supposed to go, there was white space.

In the middle of the white space, in the smallest type font Adam could find on his computer, was a brief message:

"The Harris principal, Mrs. Marris, has prohibited the *Dash* editors from printing the story planned for this space. Those interested in reading the banned article should go to . . ." and it gave the do-it-yourself romance website address.

Marris looked up. She seemed calm, in control. "That will be all," she said to them. "Expect to be called down this morning for your expulsion notices."

That *was* all. As they climbed the stairs toward daylight, each footstep sounded like a small explosion.

Walking along the empty corridors to home base, they heard Miss Esther's voice over the loudspeaker calling the technology aide to the principal's office.

All morning they waited to be summoned, but lunch came and went and they were still there. Every time they ran into a *Dash* person, there was a new tidbit. Someone had seen the superintendent walking into the building. Someone had spotted the board of education president in the main office.

Adam wondered why they just didn't call him and Jennifer down, expel them, and be done with it.

By the end of the school day, there was still no word.

Phoebe stopped by the *Dash* office after school. She'd left a book in 306 that she needed for a homework assignment, but the door was locked, which was odd. It never had been before. Phoebe found Jennifer at her locker, but Jennifer knew nothing about it either.

So they went down to Eddie's office. He had keys for everything. The girls called his name, but there was no answer. The boiler could be so noisy, Eddie might not be able to hear them, and they walked in.

The room looked strangely bare. Then it dawned on them. All Eddie's personal things—his family photos, his lunch pail, his black bubble winter coat, his red-and-black checked wool cap with the earflaps—all were gone.

They tried to find Adam to let him know but couldn't.

The whole day Adam had moved from room to room like a man waiting for the Grim Reaper to tap him on the shoulder. He walked with his chin thrust forward, his eyes fixed straight ahead.

His math teacher had asked if he had a stiff neck.

Adam's voluntary/mandatory teacher did a double take when he arrived early. Afterward, Adam went straight home.

He was accustomed to both his parents working and normally liked having the run of the house after school.

Today it would have been nice if there were someone at home to talk to.

He dropped his coat and backpack by the front door and moped down to the family room. He planned to e-mail Jennifer. See if she knew anything.

He logged on and checked his in-basket. There were seventy-eight new messages. His heart was pounding. He quickly scanned the subject fields. The e-mails had titles like "Way to Go," "Need to Talk," "Amazing Job," "Great Story," "Tip of the Iceberg."

Before opening a single one, Adam jumped out of his chair, twirled around, pumped his fist, took a running leap, stretched with all his might, and, for the first time in his life, touched his entire palm to the family-room ceiling.

chapter 21

Ave Atque Vale

The Wednesday morning notices were read by Mrs. Rose. All day there was a spooky public silence at school. Officially, no one said a word. Unofficially, people gossiped endlessly. All kinds of wild rumors circulated among Harris students and beyond.

One had Mrs. Marris barricaded in the Bunker with dynamite strapped to her waist, refusing to come out. Another reported that she had escaped through a secret tunnel and was now living in Argentina, where she had stockpiled massive amounts of gold plumbing fixtures.

Miss Esther seemed to have disappeared, too, and someone said they'd heard she was actually Mrs. Marris's aunt. Franky Cutty swore to Adam on his grandmother's holy grave that Miss Esther had once been a Las Vegas showgirl married to a bigtime mobster. "At this moment," Franky said, "I bet she and Marris are sitting in a comp suite for high rollers at the Desert Flamingo, drinking free brandy alexanders."

This much they knew was true: the parking space reserved for the principal was empty. During recess Sammy had sneaked around to the teachers' lot, and the red Porsche was gone.

That week no teacher said a word about any of this to Adam. Then, the following Monday, Mr. Brooks asked him to stay after class. The world history teacher remarked that he had seen one story from the November *Dash* that he called "Pulitzer Prize material" but wondered whether there were more.

"We had the whole issue ready to go," said Adam, who proceeded to fill in Mr. Brooks on the final Bunker showdown with Marris, including her threats to expel them and blacken their permanent records.

"You know," said Mr. Brooks. "If you want to print the rest of the November issue, I'm sure you'd find a receptive audience."

Two days later all twenty-three *Dash* members stood out front of Harris, handing out the paper, the smallest among them shouting the loudest. "GET YOUR *DASH*!" bellowed Phoebe. "ALL THE LATEST FRONT-PAGE NEWS!" Even parents wearing pajamas under their overcoats, who were just dropping off their kids, jumped out of their vans and SUVs to grab a copy.

Second period, Adam was summoned to the principal's office—but only because he'd forgotten his baritone mouthpiece and his dad had dropped it off. When he walked in, Mrs. Rose's head said, "Good morning, Adam," and there was an unmistakable softness in her eyes.

Phoebe had been checking the boiler room daily, and finally that afternoon came racing up to 306 to report Eddie was back. The janitor's union had gotten him a lawyer and he'd been rehired—with an apology. He was paid for the time he missed and told Phoebe it was just like a vacation except for the worry of it.

* * *

Jennifer had no trouble convincing Adam to go with her to the December school board meeting. There was a line of grownups waiting to speak that snaked halfway around the auditorium. The leadoff question was about "the Harris principal situation."

The board chairwoman explained that because it was a personnel issue, she could not discuss the matter publicly. She said that as soon as everyone in line had a chance to ask questions on other subjects, the board would go into executive session to review the case.

Everyone standing immediately sat.

Three hours later, when the board members emerged, the auditorium was still packed. The chairwoman explained that all she could say at the moment was that the current Harris principal would be taking an indefinite leave to care for an elderly aunt who recently had suffered a major shock to her system.

The search for a replacement was to begin immediately.

They'd done it and, yet, the *Dash* reporters found they had no time to rest on their laurels. It was as if every story they wrote spawned a new story—and a whole new set of worries.

They couldn't wait to see the *Citizen-Gazette-Herald-Advertiser*. They figured finally that rag had to acknowledge what the *Dash* had done. But there was not a word in the next issue. There was a report labeled EXCLUSIVE on the front page about a new principal for Harris. The story said that "according to an unnamed telecommunications magnate," the school board was "seriously considering" an assistant senior vice president for marketing at Bolandvision Cable. The story pointed out that Bolandvision always put the people of Tremble first and was willing to grant any executive a leave of absence "to save the public schools."

No school official thanked Adam or Jennifer or anyone from the *Dash*. These adults had trusted Marris, felt honored when she had confided in them. One board member told Jennifer's mother that the *Dash* had a lot of nerve tarnishing the school system's stellar reputation and said such matters should have been handled discreetly "within our Tremble family."

* * *

327

Jennifer was planning to go to the zoning board meeting in mid-December to see if there was any hoop news. But then, one evening that week, her dad hollered for her to come into the den quickly.

There on the giant TV screen was Peter Friendly, Cable News 12, saying that the zoning board's December meeting had been canceled due to "pressing holiday demands on board members." The board would meet again in January, he said. "Sources have told Cable News 12 that the accessory structure policy is going to be thoroughly reviewed by a blue ribbon commission," he added. The camera then panned to a very tanned-looking zoning board chairwoman explaining that she was working overtime to straighten out a confused public. "Apparently two overzealous, low-level Code Enforcement boobs acted in a totally unauthorized manner," Mrs. Boland told Cable 12. "Believe me, Peter, I have handled this with an iron fist."

Mrs. Boland explained that homeowners who had been red-tagged could now safely go about their business without fear of prosecution.

"This is a minor blip," Mrs. Boland bubbled on. "Our board will be undertaking several exciting new projects in the new year. We are committed to eliminating every last pocket of blight in Tremble. Big changes are coming."

To end the report, Peter Friendly said, "Mrs. Boland, I understand you have a consumer tip for removing an unwanted red tag."

"That's right, Peter." Mrs. Boland smiled. "I suggest a bucket of soap and warm water mixed with two capfuls of ammonia."

"And a little elbow grease?" Peter Friendly winked. "This has been another exclusive Cable 12 Eyewitness report."

As Christmas approached, there were holiday concerts to rehearse for, holiday basketball tournaments to practice for, holiday shopping trips to plan for. Some days, Adam's To Do list was three feet long. In room 306 unanswered questions kept piling up. Who would be the next principal? Where would Spring Boland strike next? Had they really heard the last of Marris?

Adam and Jennifer found the better the *Dash* became, the more people expected. Big kids Phoebe didn't even know spotted her in the hallway and shouted, "Yo, Front-Page, whatchya got cooking?"

Every day Phoebe raced into 306 with another

hot tip. By the week before Christmas, she had eight front-page stories working, none that she could finish in the next six months.

Finally, Jennifer had to throw up her hands and scream, "Enough!" It was time, she told her staff, to stop and smell the roses. They'd all been so crazy with the Marris story, they were going to take a break and wait until after vacation to do a combined December/January issue. Jennifer said she had researched it, and there was no disgrace in a combined issue; even the *New Yorker* did it sometimes.

The cheering was so loud, Eddie heard it in the boiler room.

The *Dash*'s annual holiday party that week was the best in memory. Everyone was in a great mood; just three days of school left. They drank punch bowls full of jungle juice, danced on the couches, and wolfed down several cartons of Sugar Booger Dips and Brown Sugar Wallops.

There were joke gifts for everyone. Adam and Jennifer got tiny toilet bowls spray-painted gold. The typist who had been so scared that night at the boathouse got a rubber mouse. Phoebe was presented with a CD they'd burned specially for her of Phyllis's screaming voice turned into a rap song:

> I knew that girl was a moron dwarf.
> When I see Phoebe, I want to barf.

It was dark by the time the party ended. Jennifer and Adam stayed after to clean up so Eddie wouldn't have a fit. As they headed out, Adam nearly tripped against something that had been left leaning against the door to 306.

He stepped back into the room and tore off the wrapping paper. It was a plaque. At the top it said *Excelsior!* And then:

To Adam and Jennifer, coeditors extraordinaire,
who demonstrated courage of mythic proportions,
marching below the earth's surface,
engaging in mortal combat, slaying the beast,
and emerging from the Bunker into the daylight,
their permanent records untarnished.
With fondest admiration,
Prescott Brooks

Adam read it twice. He was so moved, he was afraid Jennifer might see, so he looked out the window. That's when he noticed. The first snow of the winter was really coming down.

The windows were steamy, and Jennifer used her hand to wipe clear a spot. "Perfect night for Adam Canfield's one-hundred-percent-foolproof wake-up system," she said softly. Her head was so close, Adam could smell fruity apricot shampoo. She leaned toward him—then punched him on the arm and raced out of the room, yelling, "Too fast to be last!"

Adam shook his head in disgust and turned off the lights, but he was smiling in the dark.

ABOUT THE AUTHOR

Michael Winerip says that many of the stories in *Adam Canfield of the* Dash are based on his own experiences working as a newspaper reporter for thirty years. "I wanted to write a book about kids with super powers," he says. "So I gave Adam lots of notebooks and pens and a newspaper that would print his stories. Next, I threw in a few suspicious characters, then stood back and waited for some magic stuff to happen."

Michael Winerip is a Pulitzer Prize-winning reporter for the *New York Times*, and is also the author of an award-winning non-fiction book for adults, *9 Highland Road*. He lives with his wife and four children, who provide fresh material for his writing daily. *Adam Canfield of the* Dash is his first book for young readers.